The Chronicles of Avantia

With special thanks to Stephen Chambers

For Mamasan

www.chroniclesofavantia.com

ORCHARD BOOKS
338 Euston Road, London NW1 3BH
Orchard Books Australia
Level 17/207 Kent St, Sydney, NSW 2000

A Paperback Original
First published in Great Britain in 2011

Chronicles of Avantia is a registered trademark of Beast Quest Limited
Series created by Working Partners Limited, London

Text © Beast Quest Limited 2011
Cover and inside illustrations by Artful Doodlers, with special thanks
to Bob. © Orchard Books 2011

A CIP catalogue record for this book is available from
the British Library.

ISBN 978 1 40830 749 6

3 5 7 9 10 8 6 4

Printed and bound by CPI Group (UK) Ltd, Croydon, CR0 4YY

The paper and board used in this paperback are natural recyclable
products made from wood grown in sustainable forests.
The manufacturing processes conform to the environmental
regulations of the country of origin.

Orchard Books is a division of Hachette Children's Books,
an Hachette UK company.

www.hachette.co.uk

Call to War

By Adam Blade

ORCHARD BOOKS

www.chroniclesofavantia.com

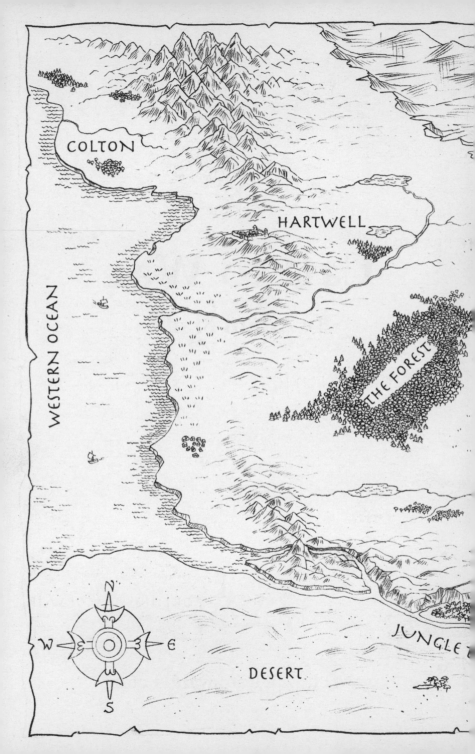

THE ICY PLAINS
Avantia
BROKEN GORGE
E PLAINS
CITY DWELLING
FORTON
COLWEIR
AIN
THE WINDING RIVER

Predators and prey

Prologue

The world is dark, but I am awake, alert. I feel alive in the night. I sit in the moonlight, listening to the forest. Branches scrape, leaves rustle, and I detect the sweat from an animal's skin and the warmth of their breath not far away. Good.

My golden brown fur covers muscles that ache to pounce, but I don't move. Not yet. My eyes adjust and filter the moonlight into a blend of green foliage and purple shadows. A holly bush trembles directly ahead of me. I smell it in the wind: a wild boar is rooting in the dirt. I am Nera, a Beast of claw and poise. Slowly, I slip forward, muscles tense like the spring of a trap. I pad closer, my mind calm, all the tension flicking in my tail. I am invisible in the night, and I am upwind. I am the hunter. I know no fear. Creeping closer, my attention is fixed on the shaking bush and the prey behind it. I am close enough now. It can't get away – I can outrun it in the chase. I am sure of it. I am no ordinary jungle cat. I am Nera, hunter.

Behind me, I hear a low chirp.

I freeze. The bush stops shaking – the boar's heard it too. My body tenses, I glance back: Firepos, my mentor, is watching me in the moonlight. A great Flame Bird, she is a Beast of terrible fire and wisdom. Now, as my vision shifts to bring her into perfect focus, her feathers shimmer red and orange. Her beak is curled and sharp, and she stares me down with unblinking eyes. She's as big as me.

I hear the boar begin to dig again. I can catch it, I know I can, but Firepos does not break her gaze. She knows something.

Behind the boar, a twig snaps. The boar bursts from the brambles, running fast. My claws curl into the dirt, I slink closer, ready to attack, and – a boy leaps out of the bushes after the boar! His sword raised, he is exhilarated, until he sees me. The youth freezes, our eyes meet, and he frowns, breathing hard. The sword is too big for him, oversized in his hands.

'It's getting away,' he says. 'You made me lose the hunt.'

I made you lose it? I step closer to him. He is different from anyone I have seen before. He doesn't cower, doesn't retreat, as I sniff and flash my teeth. I think: I am Nera, boy. You will fear me.

When I growl, he smiles. 'I am not afraid of you,' he says, 'whatever you are.'

He is too young to be this headstrong. Yet something about his easy stare and steady stance – his sword still poised – is familiar. I should teach him a lesson.

I tense, and the boy points his huge sword at my neck.

'Try it,' he says.

I pounce, and as I swipe for his head, he ducks, grabs my fur, and leaps onto my back. When I roar, the boy raises his sword and whoops a war cry. His shout matches mine, and his weight on my back feels...right.

Finally, I understand. I know why his gestures are familiar. I know them too well: they are just like mine. We are the same.

When I look round, Firepos is gone. We are alone in the woods, and as I pace in the moonlight, I catch the scent of the boar again.

'Nera,' the boy says. 'Your name is Nera. I'm Castor.'

I send him a message: We are the same. I feel his muscles

relax in understanding. Then I sprint into the foliage, and Castor laughs, surprised at my speed.

'Let's catch the boar!' he cries.

I bound faster, trailing the hot stink of the animal. We hunt the boar, then a deer, and in the morning, when he returns to his village, Castor pats my side. I feel his message strum through me: I'll see you tonight.

I purr, and one night becomes two, two nights become years with Castor on my back and beside me with his sword, until he's grown enough for its hilt to fit his hand. We revel in our hunts, in the way entire herds of goat and wild horses scatter before us. We face bears and vipers, clumsy horned cattle from the north, and we always return together. We are stronger than them.

'We'll always be together,' Castor says once, exhausted and covered in the grime of a creek bed. We had chased a clipper eel downstream for miles, finally pinning it under rocks.

That night, as I carry him home, I think, I will kill anyone that touches you. My chosen Rider, my Castor.

Riding over ruins

Chapter One

The golden chain turned slowly as Gwen held it in front of her face. Scratched and worn at the edges, the locket still glittered in the dawn light. Gwen's blue eyes were bright and focused, her white-blonde hair tucked behind her ears, still dishevelled from where she had slept on the ground. Behind Tanner, Castor was still waking up.

Their three Beasts, Gulkien, Nera, and Firepos, stood guard at the edge of the forest clearing. Firepos was a huge Flame Bird, her feathers shimmering golden as tiny flames flared at her wing tips. Beside her, the flying wolf, Gulkien, stretched his leathery wings as his lips curled back and he ran his tongue over long fangs.

Tanner could sense the message Firepos sent him across the air: *A new day brings fresh challenges.* Tanner and his Beast had been together ever since he'd been a young boy. Together, they'd survived the death of his father and the kidnapping of his mother at the hands of the evil warrior, Derthsin. Firepos had helped Tanner survive.

And we'll keep surviving, won't we, Firepos? He silently sent the message to his Beast. They instinctively understood each other, and always had.

A crow cawed. Tanner recognized that sound: the screech of a carrion bird, searching for a corpse. He waited as Gwen traced her finger around the edge of the locket, tapping a hidden button. Something clicked, and the front cover popped open.

Castor came over to see, his golden hair clumped with leaves and dirt where it curled around his temples. 'Why are we up so early?' he grumbled, wiping the sleep from his eyes.

Gwen carefully placed the open locket on a clear patch on the ground. She plucked out a tiny gossamer square that shimmered and sparkled like river water in the dim light. 'We have to keep moving,' she said, without looking up. 'Open the map.'

Tanner reached into his tunic and slowly unfurled the parchment map they had followed over the past few days. His hands steady and careful with the cracked edges, he laid the map between them. Gwen shook open the gossamer – it unfurled like a tiny sail – and she placed it over the parchment. Behind them, Tanner heard Firepos rustle her wings. Gulkien sniffed and paced, while Nera's wide cat-eyes scanned the forest canopy.

Castor sighed. 'I don't see anything.'

'Be patient,' Gwen said.

Tanner leant close to Gwen. The gossamer shimmered like a wax skin, blurring the colours of mountains and forests, smearing the lines of roads and the names of towns and villages.

'It makes things harder to see,' Castor said, craning over the top of their heads, 'not easier.'

'You know how this works,' Tanner said, still watching the map. 'It should show us where to find the third piece of the mask.'

'Right,' Castor said. 'So we can lose it like we

lost the other two pieces.'

Tanner tried to ignore him.

'Castor please,' Gwen said. 'Just wait...'

The wind blew harder, and when the overhead branches parted, a shaft of daylight lit the map. A tiny picture blotted the gossamer, like an ink ghost, as if the daylight had brightened the world just enough that they could see something that had been there all along. A small image glowed like a gemstone. When Tanner peered closer, he saw the outline of a leathery cheek and the edge of a brow – a piece of a small, empty face. Tanner shivered, but there it was, hidden near the Southern Caves. The third piece of the Mask of Death. Tanner had been tracking the pieces of the mask ever since his grandmother, Esme, had died at the hands of Derthsin's general, Gor. She'd told him to go to Jonas the Mapmaker.

They'd fought hard to snatch the pieces of the mask from Derthsin, but Castor was right – they'd failed. They didn't have a single piece – General

Gor hung the pieces from his belt, as if to mock them. The mask was said to be made from the face of the first Beast of Avantia, Anoret.

We have to get the pieces back, Tanner swore to himself. *For the sake of all that is good in this kingdom. If Derthsin gets the mask, he'll have power over all the Beasts, and then he'll be able to rule Avantia.* It may have been made up of feudal towns and villages, scraping together an existence, but it was the place Esme had loved with all her heart. For the sake of his murdered grandmother, Tanner wouldn't allow Avantia to crumble.

Gwen tapped a north-south line on the map. 'This path links the armoury – where we saw Derthsin's men making weapons and armour – with the Southern Caves.'

'They may have built the armoury there,' Tanner said, thinking aloud, 'so they could equip an army for the south.'

Castor frowned. 'I don't like this.'

As Tanner rolled up the parchment map, he

looked over the flat greens of Avantia's grassland and the darker blotches of forest that stained the centre and edges of the map. There were still so many parts of this kingdom that Tanner had never even visited, yet he knew he would be willing to fight for all of Avantia. Anything rather than give it up to Derthsin.

Derthsin. The man who had murdered his father and abducted his mother. After this happened, when Tanner was a child, he had been left in the care of Esme, who had showered him with love and discipline in equal measure.

Firepos had cared for him too, training him as a Chosen Rider. Then, the nightmare had returned. General Gor's army had attacked Tanner's village, under the orders of Derthsin. Tanner had thought that this evil, faceless warrior had died after Firepos had taken her revenge, hurling him into a volcano. *But I was wrong*, Tanner thought.

Derthsin had returned, to torment not only Tanner, but the whole of Avantia. He wanted the

Mask of Death, which would give him control over the Beasts. Pieces of the mask were scattered and hidden around the kingdom. With her dying breath, Esme had sent Tanner to find Jonas the Mapmaker. Tanner had failed. But he had found the twins, Gwen and Geffen, whom Jonas had adopted. Gwen had a secret map, revealing the locations of the pieces of the mask.

Since then, they'd travelled with their Beasts – Tanner on his Flame Bird and Gwen with her wolf. They'd met Castor in a village stripped of its menfolk; he'd been the last boy standing. Tanner could hardly believe that this preening boy with a sword and dagger had a Beast, and was chosen to fight alongside them. His arrogance had taken Tanner's breath away, and only reluctantly had he fought alongside this new friend. But they had been bound together with blood and loss during the fight in Derthsin's armoury. Gwen's brother, Geffen, had been lost to the evil thrall of their enemies, and he'd lost his life in the armoury.

Tanner risked a secretive glance at Gwen. She'd seen her brother's death. Would she ever be the same again?

Tanner returned the map to her and touched her shoulder. Her eyes were swollen from lack of sleep. 'I'm fine,' she said. She put her gossamer away and hung the locket back around her neck.

'Come on,' Tanner said. 'It's time to go.' Once he'd been a simple baker's boy; now he had a mission to stop Derthsin. He'd become a better swordsman and could think tactically now. But it wasn't just that. *I need to finish this*, he thought. Whatever Derthsin had started, he would end, or he'd die trying.

'Hang on,' Castor said. 'I'm part of this team. I think we should wait. I have better instincts and I'm telling you, we need to wait until the sun burns off the morning dew.'

'You have better instincts?' Tanner said. 'We don't have time to hang around, Castor. General Gor has two pieces of the mask.'

'And we all know whose fault that is,' muttered Castor.

Anger flared in Tanner's chest. He remembered General Gor taunting him at the mines. 'You have nothing to look forward to but your deaths,' he'd told them. He'd almost been right – there had been too many soldiers and Tanner had been helpless to steal the mask pieces from him. But in the mines, Castor had been brave, selfless – he'd helped Tanner save the boys, even though Gwen's brother had been lost. *We need that Castor, not this arrogant, disgruntled one*, Tanner thought.

Gwen put a hand on Castor's shoulder. 'Please Castor, don't fight about this now.'

Tanner went to Firepos and grasped her bright feathers to help him climb onto her back.

'We can't wait,' Tanner said. 'We have to start our journey. It's time to go.'

Castor smiled at Gwen as she climbed onto Gulkien. The wolf bared fangs the size of daggers, and leathery wings sprouted from his shoulders.

His yellow, unblinking eyes watched Castor leap onto Nera's shoulders. Her eyes blinked and she sent out a hiss, baring her razor-sharp teeth. From his position on her shoulders, Castor called to Tanner, rolling his eyes: 'Well then, fearless leader, lead the way.'

Flames flickering at my wingtips, I launch myself into the air. It feels good to stretch my body, point my beak towards the adventure ahead. As I take off into the trees, breaking for the sky, I feel an irresistible pull. I know Tanner feels it, too. We are drawn towards the next test of our strength; we cannot turn away. We approach our fates; let Destiny be kind to us.

Firepos carried Tanner up, and in a blur of smashing branches, they blasted through a hole in the canopy into the open air. Firepos cried out, revelling in her speed. Tanner gripped his Beast, but as Firepos lurched right, his hold slipped. Frantically he grasped Firepos's feathers, fingers digging in hard, hauling himself upright.

You're faster than the wind! he thought, sending a message to his Beast. He smoothed Firepos's feathers, and they shimmered with brilliant yellows, oranges and rippling reds. When he looked closely, Tanner could see the feathers flickering with the fire that burned inside them, waiting to be released. *My phoenix*, he thought, *my Flame Bird*.

'Hey!' Castor called from below. On the ground, Nera bounded over the hills in sudden, irregular bursts of speed as her golden fur rippled over tight muscles. There was no bounce or rhythm to her movements. Instead, Nera leapt from one position to the next, as if she were always searching for the best point of attack.

Firepos banked lower. They had cleared the forest, heading south. Gulkien flew with Gwen beside Firepos, and below, the Northern Mountains flattened into hills. Bulging rock turned to grassland and isolated evergreen tree copses that might have once marked the borders of estates or chiefdoms.

'Hey!' Castor called again.

'What?' Tanner shouted down to him.

'We should race!' Castor yelled. 'Nera is faster than Firepos and Gulkien put together.'

Beside Firepos, Gulkien snorted and pawed the air, his leathery wings beating steadily. 'Castor...' Gwen said.

'What?' Castor said, his face flushed. 'You're scared?'

'Stop it, Castor!' Tanner shouted. 'We need to move cautiously. You know there may be an army in the south...'

'Stop making excuses,' Castor called. 'You're afraid you'll lose!'

Gulkien growled as Nera started to run faster. Even Firepos made a low, grumbling cry.

Idiot, Tanner thought. *We may be flying right into the path of an entire army, and he wants to race.*

Nera was charging ahead, leaving Tanner, Gwen

and their Beasts behind.

'Enough!' Gwen called. Her cloak flapped open in the wind as she leant forward on Gulkien. Tanner glimpsed the rounded hilt of her rapier, a long, slender blade, and the grooved handles of her throwing axes. *She has surrounded herself with blades of iron*, he thought. Gwen laughed and pointed ahead. 'Go, Gulkien.'

Gulkien howled and pounded his wings in a sudden jolt that sent him after Nera. Castor laughed and shouted back, 'Catch up, Gwen!'

Firepos's chest rumbled again, and Tanner leant closer to her. Seeing Gwen smile made Tanner's pulse quicken. *If she's ready for a race*, he thought, *I am too*. Over the rush of air, he said, 'Beat them, Firepos.'

Firepos screeched and flew higher, her great wings of feather and flame streaking hot against the sky. Looking over his shoulder, Tanner saw trails of steam as she rose. Tanner knew that she was rising the same way a hawk circled, ready to drop in a flash of talons and deadly speed. He remembered almost losing his grip the first time Firepos had shown him how fast she could dive.

Now, as they rose higher, he watched Gulkien's shadow close on Nera. He heard Castor taunting Gwen. She laughed and called back. But ahead, the emerald farmland and distant sheep pastures were shrouded in smoke. There were smudges on the far-away roads. Tanner scrambled in his tunic for his Looking Crystal. When he lifted the opaque glass to his eye, it cleared and distant objects snapped into focus. He saw bodies, overturned carts, and slaughtered cattle, horses – even dogs. Firepos was rising faster now, preparing for her dive.

Tanner trained the Looking Crystal on the hedges and cornstalks, on the wheat fields and green, shimmering grasslands. At the edge of every plot, he saw rubble and a grey, sooty filth. He tried to stay calm, but the race was forgotten.

Gwen pulled up alongside on Gulkien and Castor abandoned his mocking shouts from below. They all sensed trouble.

Not again, Tanner thought. *Not more attacks*.

As they continued south, it got worse. Villages without walls had been gutted and left in crumbled, smoking ruins. The towns with low keeps and protective walls had been smashed completely: their walls had been shattered like piles of sticks, the wooden buildings ground to char around lonely brick chimneys, still standing. The smoke grew thicker, and now Tanner could smell it. It stank like an unnatural firepit, where things had been torched that weren't meant to burn.

Surrounding one village, he saw long sticks with bodies mounted on them, and there, along the side of a road, were skulls stuck on pikes. Crows circled the dead. A black bird sat on a wooden sign where words were scrawled in brownish dried blood:

LORD DERTHSIN
SERVE OR SUFFER

These were Derthsin's warnings to anyone who defied him or fought back.

Firepos stopped rising, and she leant back to rub her claw against a patch of scarring under her right wing. It was an old scar: an empty wound of grey-pink flesh and mottled black spots where a feather should have been. Firepos had had the wound since Tanner was a child – since a day long ago. The day that Tanner's father had been killed and his mother dragged away. Dersthin had been there, laughing from behind his mask. Firepos had plucked Derthsin up and thrown him into the flames of molten lava. He should have died. But he'd survived. Derthsin had had the mark of a feather burned into his palm – the feather he'd grasped to try to save himself, tearing it from Firepos's flesh and leaving a scar. Why was this old scar bothering Firepos now? Was it connected to

Derthsin? Tanner stroked a hand over his Beast's feathers, and tried to comfort her.

Below, Gulkien was soaring over Nera as she sprinted. The horizon was filled with black smoke. The roads were churned up and livestock left dead.

Then Firepos began to plummet earthwards, uncontrolled, as if she'd been hit. Tanner felt pain in his fingers flowing up through his Beast's feathers. Pain snapped into Tanner's temple, like knives wedged under his skull. He heard himself cry out simultaneously with Firepos. They felt the same pain. Tanner closed his eyes and saw an empty, dead face on the inside of his eyelids: a mask of skin and flesh in four pieces that had been bound together. Mocking laughter filled his ears like thunder. The sound grew louder. He knew where it came from. Dersthin.

Tanner plummets to certain death

Chapter Two

Pain clouds everything. I feel it pulsing fast with my blood. Tanner slumps against my shoulders. I feel his weight, heavy and slack – a snap of blinding pain, and I scream. Tanner cries out. There is evil behind this. The weight is gone: Tanner is gone. I spin and watch him slump off and drop towards the ground. He falls like a stone – no!

I cry out. Pain flashes again, but now I twist and dive. As he tumbles, I see his face contort with agony. Each twinge of my pain makes Tanner scream. The ground is too close. He rushes towards a hillside of hard, shallow dirt. His eyes are squeezed shut. The pain beats and burns in my limbs.

Overhead, Gulkien calls out, and I glimpse Nera rushing closer below, too far away to catch Tanner. I stretch out my talons. I reach, I grasp. Tanner's clothing flaps violently in the air, his body turning in a slow circle. The ground is nearer. I watch each instant. I reach out further until...yes! I catch him, pulling back with both wings open. The jolt stretches my spine, tests my muscles, but they hold, and we *hover. Tanner is limp in my claws.*

Gulkien approaches me, and Nera hurries below. I hear Gulkien's Chosen Rider, Gwen, arguing with Nera's Rider.

As Gulkien draws nearer, my old wound throbs, and the sudden flare of pain knocks me off-balance again. I hold Tanner, but I drop, unsteady, to the ground. Tanner shouts and grabs his head.

I cannot protect him from this. We have to find help.

No time. Now, while he is still breathing. I look up, find a straight, distant line atop a hill: a village. I open my wings, with Tanner in my claws, and rush into the air without looking back. My muscles complain, my blood strains, and as my heart beats faster, it is as if a hundred blades have lodged into my old wound. If I am to die, let it be to save him.

'Tanner? Tanner, can you hear me?'

The white hot pain faded to the edge of Tanner's vision, like ink dissolving in water. He could see blurry figures, backlit against the sun.

The ground was hard beneath his back, and there was a terrible ringing in his ears.

Tanner squinted and the figures came into focus: Gwen and Castor. Gwen's eyes were wide and anxious. When Tanner said, 'Yes…', relief flashed on her face. Castor looked worried, frowning with one hand on his sword handle.

'What happened?' Tanner said. When he tried to sit up, his vision spotted and nausea swirled in his belly.

Gwen took Tanner's arm. 'You fell,' she said. 'Are you all right? You're white as a sheet.'

Tanner held a hand out before him and watched his fingers tremble. He snatched it back, but Gwen and Castor had already seen.

'You couldn't hold a sword if you tried,' Castor muttered darkly. 'What use would you be now in a fight?'

Tanner felt a flurry of anger and tried to snatch at Castor's collar but he easily batted him away. Tanner fell back against Gwen and he heard her gasp as she felt how cold he had turned.

'Castor's right,' she said. 'This is serious. You need help.'

Tanner's breathing had turned light and rapid.

'Your lips!' Castor cried. 'They're almost blue.'

What is wrong with me? Tanner glanced over at Firepos, inspecting the old scar beneath her wing. Her eyes rolled back in her head with the pain, but when she noticed Tanner watching she folded her wing and sent a flurry of flames over her feathers. The flames puttered and went out again. Was his pain linked to his Beast's pain? Was someone hurting them both?

Nera scanned the hillside slowly, while Gulkien sniffed, his ears straight, alert for any sign of danger.

'Where are we?' Tanner said. He tried to sit up again, and this time the pain in his stomach flared into his chest and throat. He coughed hard and slumped again. Gwen squeezed his hand.

'There's a village at the top of the hill,' she said.

'We have to go for help.'

The hillside was covered with yellow wildflowers and weeds that thinned at the top, around a wall of mismatched grey and brown bricks. Tanner took out his Looking Crystal: there was a sign beside the village palisade with a crude drawing of a skull and an axe over the words, *Death to the Unwelcome*.

'We have to get the remaining pieces of the Mask before Derthsin does,' Tanner said. 'He already has two, and if we don't stop him—'

'We know,' Gwen said. 'But you're hurt, and the villagers may be able to help.'

'Look,' Tanner said, and he offered her the Looking Crystal. 'Do you see the sign?'

Gwen read the sign, then gave the Looking Crystal to Castor. 'Great,' he muttered. Firepos made a low, clicking noise at the back of her throat, and Castor said, 'Even I know what that means. Firepos is worried about you, Tanner.'

'We have to try this village anyway. There are

no other towns nearby. There might be a healer there,' Gwen said. 'We don't have a choice.' She took Tanner's arm. 'But we don't want to provoke them. I think we should leave our weapons behind. Your swords, both of you, and my axes.' Gwen unhooked her axes from her belt and went to a nearby thorn bush. Carefully, she slipped one, then the other, through the barbs. The axes were invisible in the bramble.

Castor laughed uneasily. 'All right, but it's stupid to leave our weapons behind.'

'Not all of them,' Gwen said, and she opened the side of her cloak to show the outline of her rapier, hidden inside her tunic.

'Right, if you get to keep your sword, I'll keep my knife.' Castor patted the dagger in his belt. 'Now let's go.'

'What are you planning to do, Castor?' Gwen said. 'Fight the whole village to get what you want?' Tanner unhooked his sword as Gwen helped him stand. She caught him as the ground started to sway. Castor grabbed Tanner's right arm, pulling it around his own shoulder.

'If we have to, yes,' Castor said. 'At least then we could see what medicine they have.'

Tanner nodded to an outcrop of exposed rock below. 'We'll hide our weapons behind those rocks.'

'Am I missing something?' Castor said. 'This village has a welcome sign with a big picture of an axe and a skull on it – right above the word "Death"!'

'Death to the unwelcome,' Gwen said. 'There's a much better chance we'll be welcome if we don't go in spoiling for a fight.'

Castor helped Gwen support Tanner down the hill to the rocks.

'We can cover our weapons,' Gwen said. 'No one will know.'

'It'll damage my blade,' Castor said.

Tanner laid his sword down and gestured to Castor to do the same.

Castor laughed. 'No,' he said. 'I'm keeping my dagger.'

'We're wasting time,' Gwen said. 'Tanner needs a healer.'

'Look,' Tanner said. Coughing, he picked up a black sliver of rock. It was pointed like an arrowhead, but rounded and smooth.

'Jonas said pieces like that were Avantia's first weapons,' Gwen said. 'He told me they were made by the First People, when the world was still young.'

'Made for what?' Castor said.

'Hunting,' she said. 'And war.'

'We can use these,' Tanner said, and he slipped the rock shard into the side of his tunic so that it was invisible and cold against his skin.

'If we die because of this,' Castor said, 'I'm going to kill both of you.'

Tanner smiled. 'Thank you.'

Castor hid the rock shard in his tunic and took Tanner's arm again. 'Don't thank me just yet.

I may change my mind.'

With Gwen on his left and Castor propping him up on the right, Tanner started back up the hill. Their Beasts were waiting. Her feathers rippling like waves of flame, Firepos tended to her scar, while Gulkien sniffed the air with his fangs bared. As huge as a mountain rock, he cast a long shadow down the hillside. Nera crouched motionless in the grass, her tail waving back and forth.

'Stay here,' Gwen told Gulkien. 'If we need you, we'll call.' She narrowed her eyes and Tanner could tell she was sending her Beast a second, silent message. The wolf dipped his head in understanding.

Tanner sent a message to Firepos, though he was hardly strong enough to push it from his mind. *Wait for us.* A message vibrated back through the air towards him: *I will always be here for you.* He could see that the great Fire Bird was still in pain, just as he was. *Who's done this to us?* But this time, no answer came to him from his Beast.

Firepos took off. The wind created by her powerful wings slammed them all backwards, flattening the grass and flowers. Gulkien's wings snapped out. He ran, kicking up a cloud of dirt, and lunged into the air after her, and they were gone in the low clouds. When Tannner looked, he only saw the golden flash of Nera's fur as she disappeared around the edge of the hill.

'We're not alone,' Tanner said. 'Our Beasts will watch over us.'

'All right then.' Castor sighed. 'Let's get this over with.'

Gwen comforts Tanner

Chapter Three

I see every speck of mist as I fly through this cloud. Droplets shimmer and shine like glass beads in the air, but when the wind blows, the knives of pain are back. I glide beside Gulkien, and now he must sense it too: my hurt hasn't gone away.

The old scar, a wound inflicted on me by Derthsin many moons ago. As we circle, I watch the Riders hike up the hill to the silent village. From the air I see only a checkered confusion of rooftops. The villagers are hiding.

Everything about this is wrong. The wind shakes my feathers, and my scar throbs again. Tanner should not have to suffer my pain, but somehow it has soaked through me into him, like a restless illness.

What's that? I hear screaming and maniacal laughter. That voice brings memories flooding back. I am flying in darkness over a round mouth of red fire. The volcano boils and bursts with flame and molten rock. Derthsin, the evil one, calls out as he clutches my feathers. Shouting, cursing. Even when I shake and claw and bite at him, even when I roll back, then violently forward, and the feather tears *from my side, spraying his face with my blood, dropping him into the open, burning lava – even as he falls to his death, he cries out angrily...*

Gulkien grunts, nudging me with his wing, bringing me back to the present. I am still flying with him, over our Chosen Riders. I bank with Gulkien and we continue to circle. I am here, Tanner.

At the summit, the hill levelled out, and Castor whistled. 'Well, well...'

A big black dog sat outside the village gate. The wooden doors at the archway were open. Closer now, Tanner saw smaller pictures – crude, severed heads and hands – drawn around the edge of the wooden sign: Death to the Unwelcome.

As they approached the gate, Tanner pulled back. 'Look...' A row of jawless skulls was mounted into the bricks in the archway overhead. Under the skulls was a stone marker which read:

HARTWELL
JUDGEMENT AWAITS

Castor laughed at the skulls. 'What a welcome! I wonder how many "hearts" are doing "well" in this little village?'

'We shouldn't be here,' Tanner murmured, but when he tried to pull back, the world spun. Gwen and Castor held him up.

As they passed through the gate, a narrow dirt road led between houses with thatched roofs. The buildings were made of the same grey and brown bricks as the outer walls, and their small windows were all shuttered with wooden blinds.

'I don't like this place,' Gwen said.

'I agree,' Castor muttered. 'I'm not one to take fright...' – Tanner had to resist the urge to roll his eyes – 'but that sign over the gate. No village near Colton would warn off newcomers like that. What's wrong with these people?'

'We're a long way from home,' Tanner reminded his friends. His back ached from leaning low over Firepos's body as they'd swept above Avantia, gazing down on the burnt-out homes and destroyed farms. They'd travelled all the way to the Northern Mountains and now had swooped low over the central plains to dart further south than Tanner had ever been before. *There are no friends here*, he thought.

A dog appeared at the end of the road. Growling, it charged them.

Castor crouched low, arms out. 'Nice dog...' But the dog lunged and Castor was forced to throw himself to one side, rolling in the dirt to escape the slathering jaws of the animal.

Someone shouted, 'Enough!' Doors opened, and pale men and women dressed in blue tunics came out of the nearby buildings. The men, even the younger ones, wore full beards, and bronze charms were woven into the women's hair. They were all armed with axes, swords, and sharp scythes. Quickly, they surrounded the companions in a horseshoe shape.

'Quite the welcoming party,' Castor muttered.

Tanner was leaning heavily on Gwen's arm. He

could feel her stiffen as the villagers came closer. His vision was slipping in and out of focus, the scene before him seeming to throb with each heartbeat. He tasted blood.

'Please,' Gwen addressed the crowd. 'Our friend is hurt. Do you have a healer?'

A huge, red-headed man with a braided beard stepped through the crowd. He carried an axe over his left shoulder and wore a blue cape that was brown at the edges, as if it had been dragged in mud. There were blue tattoo lines under his eyes.

'You cannot simply enter Hartwell,' he said. 'First, you must pass a test.'

'Oh, really?' Castor said. 'And who are *you* to challenge *me*?'

Stop it, Castor! Tanner willed him. *For once in your life, rein in your arrogance.*

'I am Worrick, and these are my people. This is my village.'

Tanner called, 'Please – we don't want to fight.'

He blinked away the throbbing behind his eyes, but it came back. 'We're not here to hurt you. We—'

'Enough,' Worrick said, raising his axe. 'Our Bone Mother will read you. Hilda, come forth!'

The townspeople shifted and began to murmur. 'Another one...'

'...evil here...'

'...see it in their faces...'

An old woman stepped beside Worrick. Blue designs curled and danced on her face and hands, and when she frowned, the markings on her forehead bunched into concentric rings. Her gown was frayed blue fabric with gold tassels at the sleeves. She carried a walking stick covered in more designs with a dog's skull mounted on top. Her white hair was woven with small bones, like finger joints or bits of an animal's spinal cord. She walked towards Tanner and raised a tiny ceramic bottle.

When Tanner turned to get a better look,

his vision went out of focus: the world looked like it was at the bottom of a lake, cloudy and indistinct. He saw a weathered medicine bottle. Grandmother Esme had kept shelves heaped with pots, clay jars and miniature bottles that Tanner was not allowed to touch.

As the old woman, Hilda, leant close, Tanner saw that her hair wasn't thick with bones – it was braided into Esme's dreadlocks. Her tattoos were friendly wrinkles. Her pupils weren't cold and foreign – they were eyes he had known all his life.

'Esme,' Tanner said, reaching out for her. But his grandmother's features turned back into Hilda's, and Tanner slumped to his knees.

His eyelids were heavy. He was losing focus on everything...even his own body felt far away...

'...now!' someone was shouting. That voice was desperate and familiar. *Who?* When the voice yelled again, Tanner was backed against a wall, with the Bone Mother, Hilda, standing over him.

Gwen shouted, 'He needs your help! What are you waiting for?'

Behind her, the bright glint of metal made Tanner's head ache: the villagers were drawing their swords.

'Quiet,' Hilda said, and she popped open the tiny bottle. Carefully, she dipped one finger in and drew it back: the tip was wet and green.

'What—' Gwen said.

Hilda flicked a drop onto Tanner's forehead, another drop at Gwen, and then she stood and threw one at Castor's face. He blinked and wiped his cheek.

'What is this stuff?' Castor asked, his upper lip curled in disgust.

Hilda put the bottle away and held up her skull-stick. She watched them closely, her pale eyes ranging over their faces.

'They do not burn,' Hilda said at last. 'They are not witches.'

Castor burst into laugher. 'Unbelievable! The

world is falling apart out there, and you all worry about stupid superstitions! Is that what those skulls stuck on the gate are about?'

'Castor, you're not helping,' Gwen interrupted angrily.

Tanner's head was lurching. Sweat broke on his forehead, under his arms, down his back, and the fire came rushing back. He could hear Castor's angry voice and Gwen's sharp reproaches, but it sounded like he was listening to them from underwater. Worrick shoved Castor's shoulder. A fight was about to start, but Tanner couldn't move. A cry of pain died in his throat and he slumped to the ground.

Hilda is engulfed in magic

Chapter Four

Tanner's thoughts returned slowly. *Firepos, where are you? I have to go. Find the mask.*

Slowly, he blinked awake. He lay in a trestle bed with Hilda standing over him, pressing a wet cloth to his face that smelt of cinammon and lilac. The scent made his skull tingle, and when he sat up, Hilda shook her head. 'No,' she said. 'You are still weak.'

Tanner sat up anyway. 'Where am I? Where are my friends?' *Firepos!* Tanner thought. *Are you out there?*

Her message came back to him: *I am still here, Tanner. Still waiting.*

Tanner was wrapped in a fur blanket. Dim firelight flickered orange from a low firepit on the far wall, where a cast-iron pot smouldered and gurgled. Shadows played across cluttered shelves, tables and chairs. The tables were heaped with bottles, clay pots, jars of leaves, feathers and snail shells, and phials filled with coloured liquids – orange, green, blue and red.

'I am the village healer,' Hilda said, and she eased another pillow under Tanner's head. 'You are in my cottage.' She went to a shelf, picked up a phial of red liquid and returned to Tanner. 'Drink this,' she said.

Tanner wrapped his hands around the phial. 'What is it? Is it safe?'

Hilda laughed sharply, picked up an iron poker engraved with animals – wolf, beaver, bear – and poked the burning logs, stirring sparks.

'Trust me or don't,' she said. 'The thread of your life is thin and tangled.' She gave the fire a final stab. 'Do you know what your bones say?'

Tanner felt his pulse quicken. *She's mad*, he thought. But her tone, and the confident way she moved was subtly familiar. Esme had carried herself like this. He couldn't help asking, 'What do they say?'

'That your future is made of blood and fire.'

A shadow passed across her face, and she murmured, 'You need more help than I can give you.'

Hilda stared at Tanner as if she could see straight through his skin, as if she knew every muscle in his body, and could read his mind. He dropped his glance and tapped the phial. 'What is in this?'

'It is destined for you. I have seen it many times in the bones. You must drink it, or you will fail.' Her face was impassive, but her eyes were alight with emotion. 'People may lie, but the bones never do.'

Tanner remembered Esme saying something similar. 'You made this?' he asked.

'No. Many winters ago, I bought it from a traveller: an old, bearded man, following the southern road.'

'Who was he?' Tanner persisted.

The woman's face coloured and she turned her back on him. 'I have nothing more to tell,' she said over her shoulder. She lifted another log onto the fire. 'Does it matter where it came from? All you need to know is that it will help you fight the enemy growing in your heart.'

Tanner rolled his eyes. *Talking bones and magic potions*, he thought. The same nonsense Grandmother Esme had trusted. She may have been right about the threat to Avantia, but he still didn't believe that the world could be cured by flower petals powdered into bottles.

It was almost as though Hilda read his thoughts. She turned and gazed at him closely. A shudder of fear passed over him. *Don't offend this woman.* It felt important not to make her angry. He found a cork stopper on the bedside table and pocketed the phial.

Hilda turned around. 'You were not raised in these parts,' she said.

Startled, Tanner noticed Hilda's eyes reflected in a glass bottle on the mantlepiece. She had been watching him the whole time: had she seen him roll his eyes?

Tanner weakly moved his body to perch on the bedside. 'No,' he said. 'I am from a village called Forton – many miles from here.'

'How many miles?' she asked.

Tanner thought. He had no idea. Flying so high above the land, without the aid of a compass and only rare glimpses of Gwen's map... It was impossible to calculate the miles. But he was far from home.

'I'm not sure,' he admitted. 'But many days' travel.'

The woman's eyes widened. 'I've only travelled that far once in a lifetime,' she admitted. 'What did you do in Forton?'

'I worked at the bakery,' Tanner said. He remembered the smell of fresh-cut wheat and rising yeast. 'I helped to grind the wheat, tend the ovens.' *And I saw all of it ruined*, he thought. 'The village is destroyed now. That's why I'm here. General Gor came with his soldiers, and it wasn't...it wasn't a battle, it was a massacre.

Derthsin ordered them to kill everyone.'

At Tanner's mention of Derthsin's name, Hilda's face whipped round. She was shaking, her eyes narrow and angry. 'Those are lies,' she snapped.

Tanner shook his head, surprised. 'You must know that Derthsin's evil is spreading. His men butchered my entire village.'

'No more!' She clapped her hands. 'Why do you blaspheme? I saved you. You owe me your life.' Hilda grabbed her skull-staff and rapped the floorboards.

Tanner backed off the bed and raised both hands. 'I don't understand...'

'You will not spread lies about Lord Derthsin, not here! If you say one more word against him, I will cut out your tongue and nail it to the doorplank – then hand you over to Worrick. Lord Derthsin protects us. Don't you see? The threat to Avantia comes from the witches that plague the land. They tear down walls and transform men into animals. We are helping Lord Derthsin to clean the land of witchcraft! Only he keeps us safe.'

I don't believe this, Tanner thought. *Derthsin's agents must have created these lies to control the villages he can't immediately seize. The people are being divided. They've been turned against each other – neighbours suspecting neighbours – so Derthsin doesn't even have to use his troops.* Paranoia and rumour were tearing communities apart, making them turn on each other, and strangers. *I have to get out of here*, Tanner realised. *Now!*

The door banged open, and Tanner and Hilda both jumped. Castor and Gwen came in, bundles of firewood tucked under their arms. Their faces were red, and Castor's hair dripped with sweat. His dagger's handle could be seen poking out of his belt and Tanner threw him a warning look.

Gwen smiled at Tanner. 'You're up!' She put down her firewood and ran to hug him.

Castor dumped his wood by the fire. 'My fingers are full of splinters,' he grumbled. 'Anyone would think I was a pack mule.' He adjusted his tunic so that his dagger was hidden again. 'Where do you want these? On the floor, Hilda?'

Hilda watched them, her eyes shining with pleasure. 'So I have you all together finally. In private,' she whispered, almost as though she was speaking to herself.

Tanner shared a glance with Gwen and Castor. 'What do you mean?'

She didn't respond, but smiled at some secret. 'Ready, master,' she hissed. Then her eyes rolled back, and her shoulders began to twitch. The air sucked in around Hilda.

Tanner said, 'We have to—'

Green fire exploded around Hilda's feet, jolting the room – Tanner caught Gwen's hand. Bottles and pottery smashed, and the wooden wall supports groaned. The green flame was spreading, curling around Hilda's legs, higher – to her waist. There was no heat. This wasn't natural fire. Without thinking, Tanner reached for his sword, but it wasn't there.

Hilda's hands clasped the skull-staff. She closed her eyes as the fire rose to blanket her torso and shoulders.

'Tanner!' Gwen called. 'What do we do?'

Surrounded!

Chapter Five

'Get out of there!' Castor shouted to Tanner and Gwen.

As the fire consumed Hilda's face, it flared white, blinding Tanner. He felt the phial grow warm inside his jerkin. He pulled it out, and saw the red liquid glow brightly. *Not river water, then*, he thought.

The firelight rose and grew, touching the ceiling, and Hilda's outline contorted through the glare. She groaned softly as the fire hissed and bellowed louder, making the walls tremble. Her shoulders popped, her arms bulged and gave, and her body swelled like a tree sprouting too fast. *She's been taken over*, Tanner realised. *Someone or something is inhabiting her body. But who?*

The white-green flame flowed out, swallowing the walls and licking at the edges of the windows and doorframes around them. The entire cottage was alive with hissing, cool flame, and as the light dissolved around Hilda, Tanner saw that she was gone. In her place he saw a tall man in a dark, hooded cloak, his face barely visible: Vendrake, Derthsin's servant! Tanner remembered him.

Vendrake's skin was bloodless, white as bone around the sneering scar that disfigured his lipless mouth and snaked down his neck. His eyes glowed pale yellow, and now, as the fire cleared, Vendrake's voice rose like a hyena's cackle. He raised a long, barbed whip and looked down to the floor, his grin revealing blackened teeth.

There was a boy at Vendrake's feet, cowering and shielding his face. Ragged and bloody, one of the boy's legs had been twisted backwards. The thorns in the whip dripped blood across the floorboards. Vendrake snapped the whip onto the boy and yanked it, ripping skin from his back. Castor winced.

'Get up!' Vendrake shouted, and he struck the boy with the barbed cord again. He pulled the whip, flipping the boy onto his back.

Gwen screamed. 'No!'

It was Geffen, Gwen's brother. His eyes stared lifelessly as his mouth hung open.

'You belong to Lord Derthsin, alive or dead,' Vendrake said, 'and you're most definitely dead now, boy.' He spat viciously onto Geffen's corpse. 'Where is it?'

'Leave him alone!' Gwen lunged at him, her rapier already aimed. Vendrake spun, and a curl of green flame blasted her back. Gwen hit the bed hard and went down. Tanner grabbed her hand, and Gwen murmured, 'I'm all right...'

Vendrake only smiled, his expression terrible and crooked, and turned back to Geffen. Geffen's arm moved. Slowly, his joint twisted and he pawed the ground. As he started to sit up, cuts were made visible on his back and chest.

'Where is the third piece of the mask?' Vendrake demanded, and as Geffen's head rolled forward, Vendrake knocked him back down with the whip.

Geffen moaned, spluttering blood. Vendrake beat him, laughing again. 'Tell me where it is or I will bury you to the neck.' He paused and turned to face Tanner, his eyes glowing and empty. 'Do you understand? This is what happens to anyone who stands against Lord Derthsin. He wanted you to see for yourself.'

Tanner tried to speak, but nothing came out.

Vendrake raised his whip again.

Gwen screamed, 'Stop it!', and when Tanner tried to hold her back, she shook him away.

Vendrake cracked his whip at Gwen: she dodged, but lost her footing, and Vendrake grabbed her wrist, yanking her towards him.

'No!' Tanner shouted. He swiped his shard of flint at Vendrake's throat who ducked, as Castor stabbed him in the back. Vendrake snarled blood, and as he turned on Castor, Tanner caught Gwen's hand and pulled her free. Castor backed away, his dagger still ready.

His breathing wet, Vendrake glared at Tanner.

'The next time we meet, I will break you. This world belongs to my master. Next time, you will *die.*'

The room flashed white: Vendrake and Geffen were gone. The flames sucked back into the floorboards at Hilda's feet, scattering pots and bottles. Hilda was crouched at the bedside, the skull-staff shaking in her hands. The room was suddenly much darker. Tanner grabbed a table to regain his balance. Castor was poised near the fireplace, his hair slick with sweat.

Tanner felt unsteady. *If Derthsin's agents had this kind of power to possess people, they might be anywhere,* he thought, *or anyone. Who could they trust?*

With a trembling hand, Gwen found her rapier. 'Geffen...what are they doing to him?' She scrambled towards the old woman, ready to lunge. 'You'll tell me, or I swear your blood will stain this floor!'

Just in time, Tanner managed to grasp hold of Gwen's cloak and draw her back into his arms.

'That woman's dangerous,' he whispered in her ear, gripping her to him. 'This whole place is. Don't attack, not yet.'

The fight suddenly left Gwen and she fell to her knees. 'Why?' she asked. 'Why is Geffen being tortured? We saw him die.'

Tanner's glance met the medicine woman's eyes. She was climbing stiffly to her feet with her lip curled in a sneer.

'Good question,' he said. Then, in a louder voice: 'How does Vendrake have a hold over you? Why do you allow him to inhabit your body? Don't you care about what's happening to that boy?'

A muscle twitched in the corner of the woman's eye. 'How does he control me? How do you think – through magic!'

'You haven't answered my other question,' Tanner said. 'Don't you care about that boy being tortured, even beyond the grave?'

The woman shook her head impatiently. 'Not if it's in the name of Derthsin. His will is iron and it is our duty to bend to his wishes. That boy must have been disrespectful. Vendrake is only giving out the punishment he surely deserves.'

Gwen whipped round, the blood rushing to her face. 'You want to know about punishment?' she said, her voice dangerously low. Tanner helped his friend pull her cloak across her body, sending a silent message not to use her rapier. She looked at him, then gave him a reluctant nod of understanding.

Castor broke the tension. 'We have to get out of here – now,' he announced. 'We don't know what Geffen will tell Derthsin, even in death.'

Hilda's face twisted, and her eyes flashed wide and angry, as she drew herself up. 'You!' Hilda struck Castor with her staff, knocking him backwards. 'How dare you slur Lord Derthsin!'

Castor was right. It was too dangerous to stay here. Any more of this hysteria and they'd be lynched. Tanner pressed between Castor and the woman, his flint shard raised. 'Step back, Hilda.

We're leaving!' He pushed away from Hilda and out of the door. 'Now.'

Castor and Gwen followed, but Hilda was right behind them.

'Witches!' Hilda screamed. 'Evil blasphemy! Stop them!'

Tanner pointed at the village gate at the end of the street. 'That way!' he shouted. It was a long way off, but they could make it. Tanner could feel his strength returning and the pain behind his eyes subsiding. 'Run!'

Hilda's shouts brought the villagers out of their houses. They sprinted after the companions, swords already drawn. 'Bar the gate!' someone yelled.

Worrick strode out of a side alley, blocking their path. He pivoted and raised his axe with both hands as they ran closer. When they reached Worrick, Castor broke right as Tanner ran up to him. Worrick swung for Tanner's throat. Tanner dived to the left. The axe missed and, as Worrick spun to follow, Gwen clipped him from behind, knocking Worrick into a stumbling somersault.

But the villagers had blocked the gate. A pair of dogs charged, their fanged mouths slavering with foam.

Firepos, Tanner thought. *Now, I need you.*

The dogs were closing in on them, the villagers right behind, and Tanner glimpsed Worrick getting back up. In another moment, they would be surrounded.

Gwen drew her rapier, directing the point at a villager with a spear who lunged towards them. Castor took out his rock shard and spun it sideways, as if he were skipping it on a pond. It hit the wardog between the eyes, and it recoiled backwards, yowling.

The villagers formed a circle, pressing Tanner, Gwen and Castor back-to-back in the centre.

Worrick stepped to the front of the circle and steadied his axe. 'Kill them!' he yelled.

As the villagers surged, there was a jolting cry.

Wind buffeted the people back, and Firepos dived into the street beside Tanner. She screamed again, opening her wings in a blast of red, orange and yellow feathers that flashed hot in the sunlight. From the gate came two roars. Gulkien flew over the wall with Nera right below him. The villagers scattered, jamming the alleys, backing against the walls of houses, as the Beasts came to their Riders.

I swoop low and drive the mob back with my open talons. When they wave weapons, I shriek and open my burning wings to block out the sun. The villagers flee from my shadow. I am careful not to harm them, but they know fear. They will remember this day.

Nera flashed her teeth at Worrick, ready to pounce. Worrick's axe trembled as he slowly backed away.

'Not so tough now, eh?' Castor shouted.

At the end of the street, Hilda screamed, 'No! Stop them!'

Tanner leapt onto Firepos's back. As Gwen picked her way up Gulkien's fur, his wings cast long shadows over the terrified villagers.

Firepos and Gulkien took off, and Nera bounded over the villagers onto a rooftop. As the roof collapsed under her weight, she leapt high, clearing the outer wall, and landing on the nearby hillside. As he rose higher, Tanner saw the mob regrouping. The villagers were headed for the gate. The Beasts had frightened them, but the townspeople were armed and angry.

'We have to find our weapons,' Tanner said.

They landed at the rocky outcrop, and when they had rolled the boulders aside to recover their swords, Gwen pulled her axes from the nearby bushes. Tanner saw Worrick at the village gate: he was leading the villagers after them.

'We can beat them,' Castor said.

'Not now,' Tanner said, and he pulled himself onto Firepos's back again.

'Tanner?' Gwen said, pointing to his tunic.

'What's that?'

The phial of liquid in his pocket was glowing, as it had when Vendrake appeared.

'I don't know,' he said. 'Hilda gave it to me. She said it was my destiny to drink it. I don't know whether to trust her or not – she might have been telling the truth before Vendrake possessed her.'

As Firepos and Gulkien took off and Nera raced down the hill, Worrick shouted after them, 'This isn't over! You will suffer before the end. This is Lord Derthsin's land. Hartwell stands with the Lord of Avantia, and we will punish anyone who stands against us.'

A moment later, his voice was lost in the wind, as Tanner soared high into the clouds. *Derthsin's evil is growing*, Tanner thought. *We are running out of time*. He guided Firepos beside Gulkien and Gwen.

'Do you know where we're going?' he asked.

Gwen opened her locket again and unrolled the parchment map, working with the gauze film as the breeze fluttered it in her hands. 'The Southern Caves,' Gwen said, and she checked the rolling hills and river, where Nera kept pace below. 'We're going the right way.'

A deadly confrontation

Chapter Six

I soar into the air, away from the hill, over a valley of shadowy pastures and rockbeds. A moment later, Gulkien and his Chosen Rider are flying beside me, and Nera leaps and dashes below.

My strength has returned – but for how long? I dare not worry Tanner; I must shield these thoughts from him. There is too much we have to do. Each time I beat my wings harder, dull pain throbs in my old wound. Tanner's strength has returned, for now, but my scar still hurts.

We fly over farmlands marked by stone walls and hedges. We follow a stream teeming with pink salmon until it joins with the Winding River and loops further south. The clouds are low and cast long shadows over the hills below. Wild horses roam in the grass amid the ruins of a trading post that has been burnt to a blackened outline. There are bodies on pikes at the crest of a nearby hill. I have never seen Avantians relish in each other's death in this way.

Tanner shouts to the others over the powerful beat of my wings. I see it too: a column of ten soldiers moving up a hillside. Below, they are leaving the wreckage of a merchant caravan. Slaughtered horses and oxen lie with the overturned, smoking wagons. The fires are still fresh, and the body of a bearded man lies with those of a woman and two children.

Beyond these bodies lies another – a man, blood spilling from his throat. A woman is being dragged away, kicking her heels against the soldier who carries her over his shoulder. My heart squeezes tight with pain and a memory of Tanner's parents comes flooding back. This is like a mirror image of the day his father and mother were torn from him. The moment I think this, I feel a response come from Tanner – I feel his pain and fury: I see it too, Firepos.

There are more bodies of men in the surrounding field – guards, hired to protect the caravan. The ten soldiers wear black armour and ride varkules – ugly, hyena-like animals with a stripe of black fur running up their spines, grimacing and slavering. We have met these animals before.

Tanner tells the others that they must intercept. They look reluctant, but do as my companion says. We descend.

If this is what Tanner wants, I shall join his fight.

Castor has already drawn his sword. Nera bounds faster.

The taste of smoke and ash makes my blood rise. I hear Tanner draw his sword, and I scream a war cry that makes two of the soldiers glance into the sky. Their varkules howl.

I draw my wings close and angle my body forward to dive. The ground speeds up towards me, and I clear the wrecked caravan with Gulkien beside me. As Nera leaps the burning wagons, the soldiers spin and regroup. The soldiers at the back ready their throwing spears, while the ones at the front aim crossbows. The varkules wheeze and snap as we close on them.

A soldier cries out an order and crossbow bolts streak towards us.

Tanner shouts, 'Now, Firepos!' I can feel the fury throbbing through him, out of control.

Heat rushes out of me, catching in my talons: I conjure a fireball and hurl it at the soldiers. Arrows incinerate in its path, and the ball of flame explodes in their centre.

Soldiers wheel in every direction, varkules shriek, and Nera and Gulkien crash into them from either side. I am a Beast of flame and speed. I dive, my talons open and grasping. I hook a soldier through his visor, grab another's varkule, and Tanner stabs the rider in the gap between his breastplate and helmet. Nera bites a soldier's head, shaking him like a rodent, while Castor twists his sword to disarm another and parry a third.

On the other side, Gulkien tears a varkule in half with his jaws, and when another leaps at him, he swats it out of the air, crushing the rider as they fall. When a soldier runs, Gwen hits him in the back with an axe. She ducks an incoming spear, and as Gulkien snarls and leaps at the thrower, Gwen whips her second axe into his chest plate, killing him instantly. Here, a varkule snarls – I split its skull with my beak – there, Tanner cuts down another soldier who is aiming a crossbow at Gwen. Soon, it is over.

Tanner wiped blood from his face as Gwen walked through the carnage to recover her axes. She planted her foot on one soldier's body and yanked an axe free.

'Woah!' Castor shouted, and Nera bounded beside Firepos. 'Well done!'

But Gwen didn't join in with the celebrations; her face was clouded with unhappiness.

'What are you doing?' she asked, gazing into Tanner's eyes. 'We cannot afford to help everyone we see. We're on our way to the Southern Caves, remember – for the mask? This type of thing is happening all over Avantia and we can't stop what we're doing every time we see a battle.'

Castor hid his dagger back in his belt. 'She has a point, Tanner,' he said. 'You know me, I love a good battle, but it's the mask we're after, and Derthsin.'

Tanner turned to gaze back over the field where he'd spotted the slain man. The woman was nowhere to be seen now; dragged away – to where? Was she still alive?

'There was a soldier over there,' he said, casting a hand out. He felt foolish now that he had to explain. 'What he was doing… It was like the day my father was killed and my mother taken. I can't explain it, I just didn't want history to keep repeating itself. I had to step in.' He hung his head. Why did he feel so full of shame when he'd just helped defeat another section of Derthsin's army? Wasn't that what this was all about?

Clouds skudded across the lead-grey sky. Firepos was making gentle noises in her throat and the other Beasts watched the three friends carefully. Castor was frowning and Gwen reached out to place a hand on Tanner's arm.

'I'm sorry for what happened to your parents,' she said, 'but this fight is no longer about them.'

Tanner caught his breath and looked into Gwen's eyes. 'How can you say that?' The blood was still slick on his hands and he bent to tear up a handful of grass to wipe the stains away.

'We have to be strategic!' interrupted Castor, his eyes glowing. 'Isn't that what being a fighter is all about? Brains as well as brawn?'

Tanner laughed with shock. 'I don't need *you* to tell *me* that!' he snapped.

Castor folded his arms. 'Well, it looks as though you do,' he said, his tone mocking.

'Enough!' Gwen didn't even bother coming to stand between them – she was already striding over to her Beast. 'Come on. From now on, we focus on Derthsin and the Mask of Death. Agreed?'

Tanner and Castor shared a long glance, neither willing to give way first. Then they reluctantly spoke as one: 'Agreed.' Gwen was right; she was always right.

'This must have been a scouting party for the main army,' Tanner said, as he climbed back on Firepos. 'General Gor may not be far away.'

'So let's get going,' said Castor, astride Nera. The Beasts let out grunts of agreement.

Firepos took off, followed by Gulkien. Nera ran up the hillside, picking up speed, and leapt off the other side. Tanner tightened his grip on

Firepos's feathers. Blood still covered his hands. Tanner's arms trembled as he wiped the blood from his skin.

Gwen gestured to the ground, her eyes wide and uncertain. 'Tanner, can you see...'

He followed the direction of her gaze through the Looking Crystal. The milky glass cleared. Below, on the bank of the Winding River, was a crowd of people dressed in the blue tunics of Hartwell. They were surrounding someone near the water. Varlot: another of Derthsin's creatures. The surface of his skin was etched with cracks; each time they met him, Varlot grew larger. His face looked different, it looked more human.

'It looks like we were right to stop here, after all,' he called to the others. Firepos shrieked and dived, with Gulkien right behind. Nera was closing on the crowd, and Tanner saw Castor smiling, both hands on his sword.

Tanner spotted something and pulled back on Firepos's neck feathers. As she slowed, he called out loudly. 'Wait, Castor!'

The people were moving towards the river. Gwen called, 'They have a prisoner! Castor, stop.'

Nera slowed, and Firepos landed beside her. Gulkien hit the ground at a run, his fangs bared and bloody. Varlot pushed to the front of the crowd. Through the press of people Tanner saw a circle of men in blue robes holding a girl with a rope around her neck. *They're Hartwell villagers*, Tanner realised. The girl's hands were tied behind her back. With swollen eyes, she looked from the fast-moving river to Tanner and the Beasts.

'They must think she's a witch,' Tanner muttered. 'They've brought her here to be drowned. They've all grown so frightened, they'll attack one of their own!' Nausea squirmed in Tanner's stomach. 'We saw how paranoid they all are.'

Varlot's armour clicked and scratched as he stepped out of the crowd. He was larger than when Tanner had last met him, standing two heads taller. Would he grow any bigger? A flickering intelligence seemed to burn in his eyes that Tanner hadn't seen before. *Is he thriving on Derthsin's evil?* Tanner wondered. General Gor was nowhere to be seen. Had he sent Varlot ahead? Is that how much the Beast was growing and changing? Could he be trusted to dish out destruction alone, now?

Turning on heavy hooves, Varlot swung a whip around slowly.

Castor said, 'We should kill him.'

Nera coiled, ready to spring, her tail flicking the air.

'They could hurt the girl,' Tanner said. 'Varlot is a powerful enemy. It isn't that simple.'

'I think it is,' Castor said.

Varlot made a low gurgling noise that became scratchy, disjointed words: 'You,' Varlot said, looking directly at Tanner. 'I know you.'

His voice was a rumble of uneven sounds, but Tanner understood it. The last time he had seen Varlot, the noises had been growls and grunts, not words. Varlot was changing.

Gwen paled. 'I understand him.'

Castor nodded, frowning. 'Me too.'

'You hear?' Varlot said, and he stomped his leg impatiently. 'Yes? Then I tell you. Go away, fools.' Tanner could see hard muscle in the spaces between the joints in Varlot's armour. 'Go!'

Tanner braced himself before replying. 'No.'

Varlot waved the whip towards the crowd, dragging crisscross lines in the dirt. 'They find evil in her,' he said. He gestured to the bound, frightened girl.

A murmur went through the crowd. The villagers watched Tanner with angry, dangerous eyes. He heard the words: '...kill...bleed...punish.'

Gwen's eyes were wide with horror. 'They're going to kill that poor girl.'

Varlot erupted into a rumbling laugh.

Castor muttered, 'I've heard enough.' He jumped off Nera and stalked closer.

'No,' Tanner said, putting a hand on Castor's

shoulder. He turned to the crowd and raised his voice. 'There are no witches here! The only evil is that of Derthsin. Don't you see that his lies have made you turn against innocent people? Look around you – this is madness!'

But the words '…lies…outsider…kill…' still floated on the wind.

Two men grabbed the tied girl and she screamed. 'No, please! I'm innocent! Don't…' With an angry shove, she was pushed into the river. She kicked and flailed, and the men wrestled her face down into the frantic spray. The crowd pressed in, readying swords and spears. 'Come closer!' a man shouted at Tanner. 'You are next!'

With a roar, Castor shoved past Tanner. He drew his sword and advanced on Varlot.

Tanner gave chase. 'Castor—'

'Varlot?' Castor shouted. He aimed his sword point at Varlot's face. 'This is for you.' Varlot cracked his whip – Castor jumped past – and Varlot yanked the whip back, snaring Castor's ankle. The whip swept Castor's feet up, knocking him onto his back. Nera snarled and charged but she was too far away.

Tanner was already running. *You're going to get yourself killed, you brash, unthinking...*

The people beside the river had started to back away, frightened by the viciousness of the fight. Varlot raised a hoof to crush Castor's ribcage, and as he began to stomp, Tanner dived with his sword. He stabbed between the armour blocks on Varlot's thigh and twisted in midair, dragging the sword all the way around. Varlot screamed and bucked.

Tanner's sword severed tendons and muscle in a bloody spray. Varlot slumped, his leg bleeding and useless. Nera crouched beside Castor, growling. Her eyes flashed angrily and a huge, clawed paw raked the air, warning Varlot to keep his distance. But the evil Beast was bent over his own injury, chest heaving as he held a fist to the flow of blood.

Gwen approached behind them, an axe in each hand.

'I think you cut his muscle,' Castor said to Tanner, panting. Blood streaked down Varlot's armour. 'I don't think he can...'

But as Tanner watched, the torn skin on Varlot's bloody thigh closed together, until the wound was a narrow gash, then a line, then gone. His breathing had calmed and he lifted his fist away, stretching his leg to test it.

'I don't believe it,' Castor muttered, pushing a golden lock out of his eyes.

'Just like Firepos,' Tanner said. He turned to look from Gwen's face to Castor's. 'How can we stop a Beast that can heal itself?'

'It's more than that,' Gwen said in a shaking voice. She pointed over Tanner's shoulder and he whirled round as faint cries of alarm sounded from the crowd beside the river. 'Varlot's growing.'

Varlot grows more powerful

Chapter Seven

Tanner and Castor backed away as Varlot's legs bulged and his muscles thickened. There was no way past him to the girl in the river. *No*, Tanner thought, *this can't be happening.* Varlot was expanding fast, his skin spreading over giant bones and limbs. As the evil Beast balanced on his hind legs, he rose higher than ever. Even his armour looked new, glowing like a polished statue.

'What's happening to him?' Gwen gasped.

'I don't know, but it's not looking good for you two,' replied Castor. 'I can keep him off, but...' He threw a doubtful glance towards Tanner and Gwen.

'Oh, shut up, Castor!' Tanner said. 'Can't you see? Every time he survives another fight with us, he's getting bigger and stronger. It's like Derthsin's repaying him or something.'

'Fools,' Varlot said, his head whipping round to face them. 'You are helpless.'

Gulkien growled and bared his fangs, stretching his wings wide. Nera stalked closer, poised low to the ground, her massive tail skimming the air. Firepos took flight, shrieked a piercing war cry and circled over Varlot, her talons open and ready, flames flickering at the tips of her wings. Tanner saw Firepos's proud eyes, glittering in the daylight. Anyone left beside the river was running towards the horizon, terrified by the sight of Varlot growing before their eyes. All but two of the men abandoning the girl they had come here to kill.

We have to stop Varlot, Tanner thought. *Firepos...*

I will fight by your side. The Flame Bird's words echoed back to Tanner. *But what of the girl?*

Firepos was right. 'One of you!' Tanner said to the others. 'Go and save that girl.'

'I feel for her, but I'm not leaving a fight against Varlot!' Castor replied, full of outrage.

Gwen shook her head. 'I'll go. If you think you can...'

'Just go!' Tanner told her. There was a flash of her cloak, and an axe flew through the air towards Varlot. As he cried out and crouched over the wound, she slipped past the huge Beast towards the river, her cloak billowing. She called back a final message to her friends: 'The Beasts,' she said. 'They're attacking!'

I fall on the unnatural Beast, Varlot, with my claws, shrieking into his face. My talons scratch at his mask, slipping and scraping, but I cannot find purchase; even as I hook the edge of his eye socket, he twists free and swings a giant fist. I dodge and come at him again. Nera attacks his back, while Gulkien springs for his legs. The air is thick with a foul taste. I can smell Varlot's flesh as he grows larger. He is a Beast of filth and treachery. His magic infects the air like the stink from an open grave, but somehow his armour spreads to hide his hulking skin and muscle. Gulkien sinks his teeth into Varlot's leg, slipping and losing his grip, as Varlot roars and kicks — just missing Gulkien's skull. Nera slashes and wrestles on

Varlot's back, her claws finding holes in his armour, but when she draws blood, Varlot swings his whip – Nera leaps over the coil – and his wounds close. He is twice our size now.

Varlot raises his whip to strike Gulkien and I close my talons on his hand, pecking the gap in his armour-joint; my beak slips deep into his flesh, and he drops the whip. He swings his other fist, and I bolt back out of reach. Nera is on Varlot's back again, but still Varlot blocks Tanner and Castor, and now, as Gulkien climbs to his feet, Varlot laughs in a ragged gurgle. He is still growing. He picks up his whip. Soon it will be too late. We cannot win, not like this. When Nera leaps again, Varlot cracks his whip across her side, knocking her to the ground. His hoof is raised, ready to smash her skull. I dive at his face and pull heat from deep within me, preparing another fireball. Gulkien flies into Varlot's raised leg, Nera leaps free, and as Varlot's fists force me away, I lock eyes with Tanner below.

As their Beasts attacked Varlot, Tanner turned to the river. Gwen was standing thigh-high in rushing water, her cloak streaming out behind her in the current. In each hand she held an axe, the blades flashing in the sunlight. The men had let go of the girl and she was dragging herself through the water towards Gwen.

'Look!' Tanner called to the men, pointing at the evil Beast. 'That is the enemy of Avantia! That is what evil looks like. You're blind if you can't see it.'

The men murmured nervously, and Castor pushed past Tanner, waving his sword at them. 'Follow the others. Go home!' When they hesitated, Castor charged into the river like a madman, lashing the air with his blade. 'Go!'

The men clambered up the slippery banks, running for the nearby hills.

Tanner started to go to Gwen and the girl, when Castor shouted and went after Varlot again. *Doesn't he have any sense?* Tanner thought.

Varlot snapped his whip over Castor's head. Nera let out a ferocious, protective roar and pounced on Varlot's back. Varlot lunged, taking her by surprise, and she fell in a cloud of dust. Firepos dived for Varlot's face. *We'll break him!* Tanner felt his Beast say. Tanner ran forward, wanting to warn Firepos. *Be careful.* Too late – Varlot sent out a fist, connecting with Firepos below her wing: the wound! She shrieked and spun, her wings flailing.

Tanner's vision blotted, Firepos's pain flooding his stomach. He doubled over, dropped his sword. He tried to look up: a hoof blurred towards his face, and a shape – Castor – lunged and swiped it with his sword. Through bright, swimming spots, Tanner saw the flash of spinning metal as Varlot knocked Castor away, moving too quickly for the Beasts to stop him.

Tanner reached for his sword. Varlot loomed towards him on bronze hooves, a huge shadow against the clouds.

'Fool!' Varlot spat, raising a giant fist.

It's too late, Tanner thought. But as he clutched

his chest, his fingers brushed something glass beneath his tunic: the phial. *I don't have a choice, I have to try. I have to do this for the sake of Avantia. I have to trust Hilda was speaking the truth before Vendrake possessed her.* He fumbled, pulled out the cork and raised the liquid to his lips...

I taste salt and something else: a tang of iron. I squeeze my eyes tightly shut and swallow, dragging the back of my hand across my mouth.

My eyes snap open as I feel my pulse quicken, my heart beating so strongly that it's almost coming out of my chest.

What have I done?

I gaze around me with new eyes, pulling back my shoulders. The fear that flickered at the edge of my vision ever since Esme's death – it's gone. I want to do battle, to lunge with my sword and see the red trickle of death at its point. I am a warrior, ready to fight. I've never felt it so strongly.

I am Tanner, Son of Forton. I'm unstoppable.

'Come here and fight me!' I call out.

But panic comes next. This can't be right, can it? To be so brave that I'd throw myself into battle, recklessly ready to die? I slow my breathing, shift the weight of my sword in my hand. That phial contained an unnatural strength. It flows in my veins now.

Varlot reared back to face Tanner. 'Thief!' he cried.

Thief? Tanner thought, shaking his head clear. He threw the phial aside. Looking back, he met Gwen's glance. She stood in the river with the girl. Gwen had saved her, but what was the terror Tanner saw in her face? Tanner followed Gwen's stare down: the back of his hand was smeared with blood. *Blood? The phial — what did Hilda give me?* For a moment, he squeezed his eyes shut as the horror hit him. He should never have drunk the liquid. Those sensations that had coursed through him — they weren't human.

I made the wrong choice, he thought, cursing himself.

But it was too late now.

When he looked back up he saw Nera on Varlot's left, crouched in a hunting pose, ready to strike. Gulkien rose to his right, and Firepos sat directly behind him. She flapped and tested her wings as if she were still in pain.

'Beast's blood,' Varlot said. 'You drink a Beast's spilled blood!' Then he looked at Firepos and let out a huge roar of laughter.

'What do you mean? How can you know that?' Tanner asked desperately. *I can't believe it*, he thought. *I'm asking Varlot to tell me the truth about myself.*

Abruptly, Varlot stopped laughing and turned to Firepos, who watched silently.

'Can't you guess, you dumb Beast? Are you so slow? The Gathering of Five...'

How can he know about that? I feel my mind turn over as I remember. He talks of the momentous day when five Beasts gathered, back before we were first torn asunder.

Nera, Gulkien, Falkor and I gave gladly of our blood in order to power Anoret. How could we have known that our loyal leader would be torn from us? The blood once collected to give power to another... Where did it go?

I look at Tanner, hastily closing my thoughts to him. The phial... No!

Has he drunk the blood of a Beast – my blood? Does that explain the twisted surge of powers I felt in him? If so, then Varlot is right to mock. A Beast's blood should never run in a Rider's veins. I will be weakened, and Tanner is...I dare not even think it. But my Rider is no longer the boy who once sobbed beside his dead father's body. He's something else entirely.

Tanner watched his Beast writhe as though trying to escape something. He'd heard her reliving the start of her story, about a gathering of five Beasts, but then she'd closed her mind to him.

What is it? Tell me! He sent the message hurtling through the air towards her. But there was no reply. Firepos was keeping her thoughts secret.

Furiously, Tanner turned to Varlot, who reared above him.

'You tell me, then!' he challenged.

Varlot raised a fist and pointed to Firepos. 'You drank her blood. You have some of the powers of a Beast!'

Gwen had run up from the river. 'What does he mean?' she said. 'What's wrong with Firepos?'

Tanner couldn't answer her. He felt anger welling in his chest, flooding past the nausea and horror.

You, he thought, and steadied his sword towards Derthsin's creature. *I am going to kill you*. If he had the powers of a Beast, then he'd use them.

Tanner threw himself at Varlot, striking out with his sword so that the blade rang off a panel of the Beast's armour. But Tanner didn't feel thwarted; he felt a stubborn determination to carry on. Varlot sent a massive fist swinging through the air towards him and Tanner just managed to duck out of range, hurling himself to the ground. Within moments he was back up, bouncing on the balls of his feet.

'By Avantia, I'll see you fall!' he called. But even as the last words left his mouth, Varlot's eyes narrowed and his fist made a low swing through the air, cracking into Tanner's chin and sending him flying. Pain shot through his skull and he landed badly, shaking his head clear. *I might have some of Firepos's powers*, he thought, *but I'm still nowhere near as strong as Varlot*. Carefully, he climbed to his feet, listening to his body for torn muscles or broken bones. Fortunately, he still seemed able to move.

You must manage your new powers, Firepos told him. *Don't become reckless.*

Tanner sent a message back through the pain. *Hurt Varlot. Do what you must.*

Firepos silently rose above Varlot, Nera and Gulkien crept behind him. Varlot was still gloating, confident in his great strength.

A fireball immediately blossomed in his Beast's talons. Gulkien swooped onto Varlot's back, slamming him off-balance, and Nera tackled his face, claws slashing and stabbing between his armour. Varlot groaned and fought back – Gulkien and Nera leapt away – and Firepos dropped a ball of flame.

'Get back!' Tanner shouted to his friends. He, Castor and Gwen dived aside as the fire erupted across Varlot, exploding in a flash of yellow heat and smoke. The blast scorched black, smoking rings into the dirt. As the smoke cleared, Tanner saw Varlot doubled over, his jaw clenched. His burns were already beginning to fade.

'No!' Tanner shouted. 'Don't let him heal!'

Limping, Varlot ran towards a distant hill. Firepos dropped so Tanner could climb onto her back, and Gwen hurried onto Gulkien's fur, while Castor ran to Nera. Firepos flew after Varlot, with Gulkien and Gwen right behind. Still bloodied and weak, Varlot saw them coming. He dropped to all fours and ran, transforming back into a magnificent stallion. His arms became legs and he picked up speed. They followed him to the top of the hill, and on the other side, Varlot leapt high over the next valley, clearing trees and streams.

Their Beasts were exhausted, weak from the fight, and Varlot was galloping too fast. Below, Castor sat on Nera's back atop the hill, and Gulkien slowed in the air beside Firepos, their wings beating steadily. They watched helplessly as Varlot disappeared over the horizon. Tanner loosened his grip on Firepos's feathers.

'It's all over,' he called to the others. 'Retreat!'

Gwen steps in

Chapter Eight

At the edge of the river, Gwen assisted the girl up. Tanner's breathing returned to normal and his pulse slowed. The power of the blood melted away, and he felt like his normal self.

Drenched in mud and river water, the girl's red hair clung to her face in dirty streaks. She was shivering, wiping tears from her cheeks.

'It's all right,' Gwen said, helping the girl sit down on a rock beside Tanner and Castor. 'They're gone – you're safe now.'

'I couldn't breathe,' the girl said. 'They just... All I could taste was water.'

With her rapier, Gwen cut the girl's hand bindings and sliced the rope from her neck. The girl watched with wide eyes as Gwen hid the rapier, with its cross-guard like an open wolf's jaw, back in the lining of her cloak.

The girl was younger than them, maybe ten years old. 'What's your name?' Tanner asked gently.

'Isadora,' she said. She pulled away from them. 'I swear to you, I'm not a witch. I didn't speak to a demon. I never—'

'We know you're no witch,' Castor said.

'It's just the people around you panicking,' Tanner added. 'Derthsin's rumours of witchcraft are helping him spread evil through Avantia.'

The girl rubbed her wrists and took a deep breath. Her hands were still shaking. 'Thank you.'

'Do you have somewhere you can go?' Gwen asked.

Isadora shook her head, tears in her eyes again. 'My own mother wouldn't look at me. She locked me out of the house when they came for me.'

Castor balled his fists and his expression darkened. 'Who?' he said. 'Who came for you?'

'Our Bone Mother, Hilda, and Worrick, our leader. My brother, I don't know where he is – they dragged him out of the village with a rope around his neck, just like… We weren't the only ones. I saw some others drown.' Isadora covered her face as she started to cry. 'The men held them under the river until they stopped moving, and nobody buried the bodies, they just...'

Gwen knelt and put her arms around Isadora.

'It's over now.' Castor stood rigidly beside them, his chest heaving, eyes fixed on the horizon.

'Do you have anyone?' Tanner asked, shifting his gaze from Castor's face. 'Is there some place you can go?'

'Colton,' Castor said, suddenly cheering up. 'If you give them my name – tell them Castor sent you. Here!' He hastily tore off a strip from his sleeve and tapped the diamond-shaped stitching, his eyes bright. 'They'll recognise this symbol. You have to go there to be safe.' He shoved the scrap of fabric into the girl's hands.

'Castor,' the girl repeated.

'I'll draw you a map,' Gwen said, 'but you'll need food...'

'The caravan,' Tanner said. 'There might be

enough supplies back at the merchant caravan. I can—'

'I'll do it,' Castor offered.

'You don't have to, Castor,' Tanner said.

'Yes,' Castor said. 'I do. I need to.' He had already climbed onto Nera and now he turned his face away. She raced across the field, her fur rippling, and disappeared over the brow of a hill.

Need to? What does that mean? Tanner watched his friend depart. *Why had he just said that, and why hadn't he been able to look at Tanner? There's more to our friend than his arrogance*, he thought. There was darkness lurking beneath Castor's shallow waters.

Gwen had settled cross-legged on the ground. She opened a blank parchment and with a narrow quill and tiny bottles of coloured ink, she carefully sketched a map, pointing out key landmarks on the way to Colton. She was just finishing when Nera and Castor returned.

Castor tossed Isadora a satchel. 'Food and fresh water,' he said. 'It'll get you to Colton.'

Isadora slung the satchel over her shoulder and rolled up the map. 'I don't know how to thank you for this,' she said. 'If you hadn't...' She hugged Gwen, then Tanner, and waved up at Castor, who was still sitting on Nera's back. 'I won't forget this,' she said.

'You don't owe us anything, just be careful,' Tanner said.

Isadora smiled. 'Don't worry, I will. But one day I will return this favour.'

As Isadora walked away, the three companions dipped their weapons into the Winding River, cleaning them of Varlot's blood.

Gwen's mouth was set in a firm line. 'Now that we're alone again, can we talk? What we saw in Hartwell, was it real or a vision? Vendrake torturing Geffen after death, making him still fight. He was hurting him, even after everything he's suffered, keeping him half-alive...' She couldn't say the words. 'It was real, wasn't it? And what about you? It was blood in that phial, wasn't it? Is it true what Varlot said – that you've drunk Firepos's blood? I saw how you lunged at Varlot. You were desperate to kill him!'

'I feel braver, stronger,' Tanner admitted. 'When Varlot was mocking Firepos about the Gathering of the Five I was able to see into her thoughts. Well, at first I could – but then she closed her mind to me. Firepos and the other Beasts gathered with Anoret – the Beast behind the Mask of Death. They were going to give Anoret their blood so that she could be stronger for something. I couldn't see anything beyond that, but…' Did Tanner dare put his worst fears into words? 'I think you're right. I drank her blood and I've inherited some of Firepos's powers. Except the blood wasn't meant for me.' He looked into Gwen's eyes. 'There might be consequences.'

Gwen crumpled, as if he'd pushed her. 'What is Derthsin doing to us?' she cried. 'Where is this going to end?' She covered her face with both hands. Tanner could do nothing but watch.

This is all part of your Fate, came a message. *We must both accept it. Gwen, too.* Firepos was watching him from a distance, her feathers glowing with tiny flames.

'Fate!' Tanner cried, making Gwen suddenly look up. 'I'm sick of being told what path my life should take! Firepos, Esme, everyone. Why can't I choose for myself?'

Tanner looked back at Castor. So far, he hadn't said a word. *And what are his secrets?* Tanner thought angrily.

Gulkien moved to sit beside Gwen, pressed his fur against her arms, and when he made a low noise, she turned. She buried her face in his fur, and slowly her shoulders stopped shaking. Her breathing steadied, and she got up, looked at them. Gwen's face was red and wet, but there were no more tears in her eyes – they looked different, as if she were staring straight through Tanner and Castor, at something ugly in the distance. Gwen's lips set in a narrow line, unsmiling.

'Derthsin won't win,' she said quietly.

The empty way she said it made Tanner shiver. It was as if she had given up a part of herself, torn it out because it was too weak.

'No,' Tanner said, 'he won't. But we're running out of time. We have to find the pieces of the mask.' He walked with Gwen towards their Beasts. 'You saved Isadora, Gwen. If you hadn't done that...'

'Isadora is alive because of me,' Castor said.

Tanner took a deep breath and tried to stay calm. 'We all saved her,' he said.

'Oh, did we? You wanted to talk Varlot to death, while they drowned her, remember?'

'And you wanted to fight him single-handed,' Tanner said. 'Remember? You charged at him before we could work out a plan. We almost died because of you.'

Nera flashed teeth like pointed razors, and Firepos shrieked, opening her wings.

There was a hiss of metal and suddenly Castor

was holding the point of his blade in front of Tanner's face. He always had been quick. 'You're not strong enough to fight me.'

Tanner drew his own sword. 'Let's find out.'

Gwen lunged between them. She held blades to each of their throats, close enough that if they moved, she'd kill them both. The blades were shiny and grooved with concentric patterns. 'No,' Gwen said. The dead way she stared at them broke their anger. 'This stops now. You're not going to fight.'

Castor tried to smile. 'Get that away from my throat.'

'Is this a game to you?' Gwen said, and slowly, she lowered her blades. 'If you want to fight, go home. Go back with Isadora, Castor. Tanner, go and sit in your village with the graves. Go and wait until Avantia dies, wait until you see Derthsin's soldiers on the next hill or at the edge of whatever field you're working in. Wait until the sky turns black. Let him win.'

They lowered their swords. Tanner's muscles were already stiffening from the fight against Varlot.

'Come on,' Tanner said. 'We need to find the next piece of the mask. It's why we're doing all this, isn't it?'

Nera snorted and backed away. Tanner climbed onto Firepos's back. It was time to go.

I fly into the low clouds with Gulkien. Nera runs below.

Now we charge straight into the mouth of a deep blackness. The hills grow rocky again. The grass thins, and stone ruins, thick with ivy and overgrowth, litter the open valley below. This is an old country. There are many memories and ghosts here, but no one remembers their names.

As I soar across the valley, scattering a herd of deer and a flock of geese, I think about Tanner. I should have known. I sensed the gift from that old woman contained something from the past – I should have warned him somehow. My scar, the old wound, was tied to that blood. Blood collected for Anoret and stolen by Derthsin. How did he get it? But what does it matter now? All I know is that my blood flows in Tanner's veins.

Ahead, a narrow valley rises to a dark rock face, split with deep, leering holes, like empty eye sockets. The Southern Caves, where the piece of mask awaits. Atop the black rock is a ruined castle of turrets and crumbling walls. Moss and vines cling to it. We near the caves, and Tanner's fingers tighten on my feathers. The castle wall once enclosed the entire mountain summit. Now, it is slowly fading back into the natural rock: the castle's pale stone blocks, once straight and sharp, are rounded to stumps by wind, rain and time.

The wind whips strongly, and I take a deep breath. I smell rank, wet fur: Varkules. Many of them. Derthsin's soldiers are close... And there is something else, something I recognize, something ancient...

I land on an outcrop of the largest cave.

The mouth of the cave was jagged and black. As Tanner climbed off Firepos and stepped into the opening, his footsteps echoed loudly, deep into the mountain.

Our Beasts brought us here, Tanner thought. The piece of the mask must be buried in the belly of this cavern. They'd already lost two pieces of the mask to Derthsin. It was more important than ever to retrieve the third piece, lying here. If Derthsin got all four pieces, he'd have power over the Beasts – and through them, over Avantia. In there, in the dark, lay Tanner's only hope of defeating the evil warrior.

The walls of black rock were shiny, like murky glass. The cave tunnel was huge, and tiny breaks in the ceiling cast narrow shafts of daylight. Tanner could see perfectly. Castor and Gwen joined him, followed by Nera, Firepos and Gulkien. The cave was big enough for the Beasts to move freely.

'This is it?' Castor said. His voice echoed into the cave. 'The place where the next piece of the mask lies?'

Tanner glanced at the scrap of red linen around

his wrist: a reminder of Esme and times when the world was simpler. For his grandmother's sake, he could not give up now.

'I think so. We have to hurry,' he whispered. 'Come on.'

Tanner led them into the mountain. Their weapons rattled, and their footsteps seemed to thunder in the darkness. As they turned a corner, the cave grew warmer, as if they were entering a house with a wood-burning furnace. *Strange*, thought Tanner. *It's usually cooler underground*. The tunnel forked.

'Which way?' Gwen said.

Something rattled, echoing out of the right-side tunnel. Castor froze. Tanner and Gwen ran to him, the Beasts following.

'What did you do?' Tanner hissed.

Castor shook his head. 'Nothing.'

Rattle-snap. The sound brought a flash of memory to Tanner: Grandmother Esme's oracle bones. They were yellow cubes, worn black at the edges and painted with tiny, foreign symbols. She had tossed them in a ceramic plate with crushed leaves and uncooked beans. 'They read messages in the wind and dirt,' Grandmother Esme once said. 'Oracle bones are always looking for the future. We just have to learn to read them.' She had shaken the bones, made them rattle and bounce – just like the sound they could hear now.

It echoed again.

Castor reached for his sword. Gwen slipped her hands into her cloak and drew two axes, the blades angled down. As quietly as he could, Tanner pulled his sword and nodded to them. Carefully, he led them into the passage.

I don't understand, Tanner thought. *Who would search for the future here?*

We follow our Chosen Riders into the deep caves. The tunnel narrows, and Gulkien brushes against Nera. She growls and drags her claws along the floor. The sound grates, until Gulkien grunts and constricts his wings – they twist and disappear into his shoulders.

Castor glares and shakes his head at Nera.

Gulkien's eyes flick back, looking for me. Yes, I know what he senses — I can feel it too. The light is dimmer here, but I am calm as we form a line: Nera, then Gulkien, and me at the rear. Long ago, men died in this cave. I can feel death, but I am not afraid.

The floor of the tunnel drops, and there are lumpy formations on the ceiling, as if the rock had been alive once. I know we are going the right way. Someone is close.

The strange boy attacks

Chapter Nine

Tanner led the way through the darkness. He could hear Castor and Gwen running their hands along the wall. He knew that Castor kept his sword poised; Gwen held her axe low and steady. Tanner crept down the centre of the tunnel, clutching the hilt of his own sword. The close air reminded him of the armoury, of running and screaming and the chaos of falling stone. Even as the light drained, his vision adjusted, squeezing the thin light into grey and white shadows. Behind him, Gulkien and Nera growled restlessly at each other.

Gwen whispered, 'Do they know something we don't?'

Firepos hadn't made a noise. Tanner looked back at her: she was watching him with steady, bright eyes. He waited for a message but nothing came. 'Maybe,' he said. He saw a faint, flickering glow around the corner ahead.

'Oh, come on,' Castor said. 'Do you really think whoever's down here is watching for us—' A beam of blue light, as thin as a stick, flashed at Castor's head.

Tanner shoved him. 'Get down!'

The wall smashed around the light in a spray of rock and dust. Gwen ducked into the centre of the tunnel as more of the wall fell in. Rock slabs crashed, breaking in a jumbled pile. She raised her axe. Nera leapt over the rockfall, with Gulkien and Firepos right behind her. Tanner saw Firepos's wide eyes and tense, sudden movements.

Castor pulled away from Tanner, and shouted, 'Show yourself!'

Silence. Tanner could only hear his own panting breath, and the rustle of Firepos's feathers. The whites of Gwen's eyes shone in the darkness.

Castor cupped a hand to his mouth. 'You coward!'

Another beam shot at him. He dived under it, rolling, and the light flashed into the ceiling behind them. Black rock exploded down, shaking the tunnel.

'Run!' Tanner shouted, pointing to the glow of light ahead. 'That way!'

Behind them, the ceiling collapsed; the roof fissure gaped and cracked ahead of them. In another moment, the whole tunnel might fall.

Castor shouted, 'Are you mad?' The ceiling fell in a rushing black wave behind them. 'That's where the attack came from!'

'We don't have a choice!' Gwen said. 'Go!'

As the tunnel smashed around them, Firepos rushed to Tanner. He grabbed Firepos's wing and leapt onto her back in one movement. A blue beam flashed past Tanner's face, struck the wall. Rock cracked and exploded, and as Tanner neared the light, the tunnel widened: it opened into a vast, airy cavern of shiny black rock. Veins of silver ran through the black floor, and stumpy formations of white and green quartz clustered up the walls to a hole in the centre of the ceiling that opened to cloudy daylight. There was another tunnel on the far wall.

There was no sign of the Mask of Death. Instead, crouched at the centre of the cavern, was a boy.

As Tanner, Gwen, Castor and the Beasts rushed into the open space, a wall of black rock cascaded in behind them.

The boy got to his feet. His clothes were mud-streaked, and through shredded holes, Tanner could see his ribs and bony joints. Long, filthy hair hung down his face.

'Keep away from me!' the boy called, and he raised both hands, palms open. His fingers glowed blue, and as the light brightened and swelled into his palms, he shouted, 'I won't go back!'

The blue light was blinding, and Tanner covered his eyes, yelling, 'Stop!' He held a hand out and slowly approached the boy. 'We're not here to harm you.'

'I don't believe you!' the boy screeched. Blue

beams blasted out of his hands. Tanner tried to duck, but it was too late. He found himself surrounded by a halo of blue light and his feet gently lifted from the ground, until only his toes connected with the packed earth. With a sigh of air he was lifted higher in the cave, floating in midair, looking down on his friends.

Gwen screamed and Castor called out angrily. 'Let him down, for Avantia's sake!'

The boy looked as surprised as everyone else. Tanner floated weightlessly in the air as the Beasts hissed and roared.

I'll make him stop! Firepos sent a message thrumming through the damp cave air to Tanner.

'No!' Tanner called out. Firepos's powers running in his veins meant he felt nothing but curiosity as he hung in the air. He glanced to one side and shot out a hand to snap a stalactite from the roof of the cave. He brought it together in both fists, holding it before his chest, the point aiming towards the boy.

Down on the ground, the boy's smile faded. 'What are you going to do?' he asked nervously. The beam of light that he had trained on Tanner began to flicker.

'I'm going to let go of this and it will pierce your heart,' Tanner said. Then he cocked his head to one side, pretending to think. 'Or you could lower me back down and we'll forget this ever happened.'

'Do it!' Castor hissed. 'You little fool.'

Gwen was staring straight at the boy. She gave him a small, forgiving nod.

The boy began to flex his fingers, as though loosening them. The light wavered even more and Tanner felt his body sinking through the air until his feet landed in small clouds of dust back on the cave floor. The Beasts watched carefully, licking their fangs.

Tanner brushed himself off and stepped up to shake the boy by the hand. Smiling uncertainly, the boy reached out to grasp Tanner's open palm. But as his trembling fingers encased Tanner's, Tanner twisted his arm round, ducking under the boy's armpit so that he was suddenly behind him and the boy had his arm awkwardly stretched up behind his back. One tug on his shoulder and Tanner could dislocate it. He brought the point of the stalactite to press against the boy's tunic, next to his heart.

'Don't ever use your magic on me again,' he hissed in the boy's ear.

'I won't, I promise!' The boy was weeping.

Castor laughed. 'What a coward.' Gwen sent Castor a long look, warning him to be quiet.

'I can handle this,' Tanner said quietly. He waited a moment more and then let the boy go, pushing him forward so that he staggered and fell.

'It's all right,' Gwen said, bending to help him back to his feet. 'Like we said, we mean you no harm. I'm Gwen – this is Tanner and Castor. What's your name? We haven't come here to hurt you or take you anywhere.'

The boy looked past her, giving Tanner an accusing look. 'You already have hurt me.'

'Oh, come on!' Castor scoffed. 'You deserved that.'

'Who are you?' the boy asked, ignoring Castor.

'We could ask you the same thing,' Castor said. 'You almost killed Tanner.' He shrugged. 'Though some people might thank you for that.'

He's my age, Tanner realized. He was the same height as Tanner. He could see that under the filth and around the frayed sleeves, the boy's tunic was dyed blue – the same colour worn by the people of Hartwell. The tunic was ragged with holes, through which Tanner could see red welts, black bruises and ugly scabs covering the boy's back and shoulders. *This is what Derthsin's hate has done*, Tanner thought.

'Let's start our introductions again, shall we? We fled Hartwell too,' Tanner said. 'We went there for help, and...'

'We found a bunch of hysterical idiots instead,' Castor said, and he pointed his sword at the boy. 'You still haven't told us your name.'

'It's Rufus.'

Before Castor could speak again, Gwen said, 'It's all right, Rufus. Why are you here?'

'I didn't have a choice, they tried to kill me,' he said. 'Because of...' Rufus held up his fists. 'This. The magic. It just happened. One morning, everything changed – I had magic in my hands, I could channel it in my fingers.'

'And shoot it at people,' Castor said. 'And lift them up in the air!'

'I'm sorry. I thought you were from Hartwell.'

'Well, we can understand why that would make you nervous,' Tanner said. 'We've seen for ourselves that they don't like anyone who's different.'

Their Beasts moved into the cavern, circling, as if they were searching for something through narrow chinks of light from the cavern ceiling.

Rufus watched, his brow furrowed, but he didn't back away as most Avantians would. Gulkien came to the centre of the cavern, but when Gwen reached out to him, the wolf-Beast continued towards Rufus.

As the Beasts approached Rufus, Tanner said, 'It's all right, they won't hurt you...' But he needn't have bothered. Rufus reached to stroke Gulkien's snout, and when Firepos craned her head down, Rufus patted the flickering feathers of her neck. This, despite the hostility the Beasts had just seen between Rufus and the others. Gwen smiled back at Tanner and Castor.

Are they attracted to his magic – to whatever energy he has in his hands? Tanner wondered.

'Here,' Gwen said, and she opened her pack to offer Rufus a handful of dried meat and carrots. 'We don't have much, but you need to eat.'

'Thank you!' Smiling, Rufus eagerly grabbed the food and ate. While Gwen laughed and rummaged for more, Tanner noticed a black stone altar set into the side wall, beside a mound of bones. There were tiny skulls in the heap. *Rats*, Tanner thought. *Had Rufus been sacrificing them?*

Tanner went to the altar: a blue cloth covered lumpy objects on top. Carefully, he pulled back part of the cloth. A simple plate full of oracle bones – covered with blue symbols, like Hilda's tattoos – was arranged in front of a row of glass bottles filled with yellow, red, blue and silver liquids containing black bubbles that swam and blotted. Next to these was a shrunken rabbit's foot, an iron mirror with a worn, engraved handle, and a narrow, sharp knife.

'My grandmother had things like this,' Tanner said.

Rufus moved over to a rock formation. 'I have another weapon, too.' He pulled out a heavy wooden staff, carved with the jumbled scales and the head of a serpent. A curved blade was fixed to the top, like a scythe.

Tanner pulled back more of the sheet: at the

back of the altar was a coloured wooden etching – the face of a girl with long red hair, full lips and inquisitive eyes. Isadora, the girl from the Winding River. Tanner shook his head. 'I don't understand. That girl is—'

'That's my sister,' Rufus said. 'I left her when I had to flee for my life. I can only pray that she survived.'

'She's still alive,' Tanner said. 'We met her, after we left Hartwell.'

Castor said, 'The villagers—'

'The villagers let her go,' Tanner interrupted. 'Isadora is going to Colton.' He tried to put the etching back but it slipped, pulling away the blue cloth, knocking things to the floor: bottles, a beaded necklace.

'I'm sorry,' Tanner said, 'I didn't mean to...'

One of the fallen objects made him gasp. *I don't believe it.* Tanner shivered. A curl of stained leather with the outline of an eye and the ridge to cover a person's nose. He glanced at Castor and Gwen. They were both frozen, staring at the leather fragment. 'Rufus,' Tanner said, 'where did you get this?'

'What?' Rufus stepped beside him. 'Oh, the Watching Mask. It was fixed to the skull above the gate at Hartwell, to protect the village. If I'm afraid, I wanted them to be afraid too. It's childish, I know. I took is so they would panic when they saw that it was gone.'

Castor laughed as he joined Gwen beside Tanner. 'It was in Hartwell the whole time. On their gate!'

Carefully, Tanner picked up the piece of the mask. The texture was coarse, and there were black discolorations from years of rain and wind.

'I don't understand,' Rufus said. 'You act like you know what this is.'

'This isn't a Watching Mask. It's a piece of the Mask of Death,' Tanner said. 'There are three other pieces. General Gor has two of them.'

Rufus's eyes widened and Tanner noticed a

pulse quicken in the boy's neck. 'The Mask of Death,' he murmured, repeating Tanner's words. 'I've heard of such a thing.'

Tanner said, 'There's a reason the world seems to be destroying itself and why your people tried to kill you. The warlord Derthsin is using them. He has armies, soldiers and spies everywhere. If he ever gets all four pieces of the mask,' – Tanner held up the leather fragment – 'Avantia will be ruined. He'll gain control over the kingdom's Beasts and no one will be able to resist him. He's already tearing towns and villages apart. With the Beast's powers behind him, he'll be unstoppable. He will tear out whatever is good in this world and twist and torture the rest. And he'll laugh while he does it.'

'He's evil,' Castor said. He turned to Tanner. 'Can we go now?'

'Rufus, I want you to join us,' Tanner said.

Gwen nodded. 'I agree.'

'Wait a second,' Castor said. 'Since when do we

need someone else?'

'You're strong,' Tanner told Rufus, ignoring Castor. 'If you weren't, you would be dead now. We saw what you can do with your power – that could be the difference between victory and defeat.'

Castor pulled Tanner and Gwen aside. He shoved Tanner in the chest. 'Are you mad? We can't take him with us! He can't even control his own hands!'

'Don't push me again, Castor.'

'It's fine,' Rufus called. 'I want to come with you. I can't stay here, and if I can get out of here maybe I will see Isadora again.'

'You don't get a vote, Rufus,' Castor said.

'He does,' Gwen said. Her expression was hard. 'I know how difficult it is for him. No one should have to lose a brother, or a sister.'

'He's unstable!' Castor said.

'So are you,' Tanner shot back. He took a deep breath. 'His power could be important, and you know it,' Tanner said more calmly. 'Why is it that every time something good happens, you start to fight?'

'And every time you should keep your stupid mouth shut, you—'

Firepos screamed, and the cavern jolted. Tanner grabbed the shaking wall. *What is she doing? What's wrong with Firepos?*

Nera dragged her claws on the ground and roared, and Gulkien joined them, his growl rising to a hoarse howl that seemed to pierce Tanner's bones, making him shudder. Firepos scratched the stone, opened her wings; Gulkien's wings snapped through his shoulders; and Nera bounded against the wall again, swiping deep gashes with her claws. The cavern could hardly contain the three Beasts.

Gwen fell to a crouch. The cavern jerked and shook as their Beasts roared and Tanner saw Castor struggling to keep his balance. The piece of the mask flapped in Tanner's hand, as he spotted

Rufus at the altar. Bundling his precious things in the blue cloth, Rufus rushed for the rear tunnel and shouted back at the Riders, 'Come on!'

The ceiling cracked.

Tanner's grip tightened on the piece of the mask as he followed, breaking into a run. Was the mountain collapsing?

Falkor slithers in

Chapter Ten

The white-hot sound stabs into my skull. I shriek and flap my wings. Tanner and the others are running for the tunnel, and I see the new boy, Rufus, dash ahead. He hears the same thing we do. The scream is too high for our Chosen Riders to hear, but Rufus's ears recognise it.

I rush into the tunnel after Rufus and glance back. Tanner is running alongside Gwen, with Nera, Castor and Gulkien behind him. Falkor's shrill scream rises again, seeming to scrape my bones. I shriek, frustrated at the tight tunnel walls. I cannot open my wings here. We must get out. I know what that call is telling us: Derthsin is close!

The tunnel twisted and sloped up in front of Tanner and as they ran, it brightened: there was daylight at the top.

'Rufus!' Tanner called. 'Where are we going?'

The Beasts were still howling, shrieking and roaring around them. Rufus continued ahead. Either he hadn't heard Tanner or he was ignoring him. They followed the steep tunnel rise, stepping and climbing over slippery, reflective rock – into daylight.

The tunnel opened onto a courtyard of ruined stone, craggy trees and ivy. The sky was overcast. Rufus helped them climb out into the open remains of the mountain castle. Around them, high stone walls were broken in three places. Heavy blocks had been knocked free and smashed, now covered with green moss, spotted mushrooms and grass sprouts. The tops of the walls were crumbled and thick with ivy and skinny trees. The regular guard posts on the outer wall were skeletal and covered with prickly weeds. In the centre of the courtyard, the castle itself was a cavernous hollow, thick with trees, bushes, and long-hanging vines that blossomed with poisonous red-yellow flowers.

On Tanner's left, the castle had been gutted, the wall cracked open with ancient burn marks around the edges. A fire had run through the castle. A tower had fallen and lay smashed across the left-side outer wall, now green with ivy – but the right side looked untouched. The roof had collapsed and the stone face was pocked with irregular holes, but it hadn't burned and broken like the rest. *Whatever happened—?*

Red eyes stared out at Tanner.

The narrow slits inched closer to one of the overgrown windows, and Tanner reached for his sword. His boots crunched an ancient courtyard mosaic, and now, as their Beasts quieted, Rufus approached the castle ruin.

'No,' Tanner said. 'Rufus!'

Castor and Gwen saw the eyes too – the slits glowed steadily, like unnatural torches – and a high-pitched hiss snapped the air. The eyes came into the light: a serpent appeared in the window-hole. It was huge. Its wide head, bristling with spikes, was poised, steady on a body of scales that swirled with rainbow colours. The serpent hissed again and noiselessly slipped down the wall towards Rufus.

We have to attack! Tanner thought.

Firepos answered: *No. He is one of us.*

Their Beasts called to the serpent. Nera purred and Gulkien snorted, as if he were laughing. A pink forked tongue flicked out of the serpent's mouth, then disappeared inside again.

Castor backed away to the stone steps of the castle wall. 'What *is* that?'

Rufus smiled as the serpent came to his side, its scales a shiny black. Tanner saw his blurry reflection repeated in each diamond-scale. He looked dirty and tired. The red scrap of linen hung from his wrist.

'His name is Falkor,' Rufus said, and he pressed his hand to the point on the serpent's head. 'He is my Beast. Until I saw you, I thought that I was the only one, but there is a reason all of this is happening, isn't there?'

Gwen smiled and reached a hand up to touch Falkor's scales. 'What does he say?'

'He says,' – Rufus smiled – 'the girl with yellow

braids is braver than the others.'

Gwen laughed.

'Never mind that,' Castor said, taking the steps up the outer wall two at a time. 'Does he say that he's hungry and wants to eat strangers?'

'I know you're worried about me, Castor. But I can help you,' Rufus said.

'No,' Castor said, when he reached the top of the wall. 'I'm not worried about you. I'm worried about *that*.' He pointed into the distance.

Tanner led Gwen and Rufus up the ruined wall steps, careful not to slip in the tangle of vines and loose stone. At the top, beside Castor, they could see across the valley to wooded mountains, and beyond that...

'An army,' Tanner muttered. A press of bodies, most in black armour. He raised the Looking Crystal, and as he stared into it, the clouded, milky centre cleared, like smooth water. He could make out faces and a dense mass of pikes, like a thin, moving forest, and as he scrolled across the army, Tanner saw a column of men on varkules surrounding General Gor. He sat on his own brown creature, its fur scored white with whip scars. Gor wore the same dragon-snout helmet Tanner remembered from the attack on Forton. Net-bags of polished skulls were fastened to the sides of his saddle.

Tanner's heart beat strongly in his chest – harder than he had ever felt it before. *This is what I'm here for.* Immediately he felt a message push back through the air to him from Firepos. *That's right. This day is what we have been waiting for.*

The soldiers' armour was scored and scratched, patched over with interlocking chainmail and fresh iron bands. Tanner pulled past Gor to try to count the number of soldiers. Varlot was there too, tall beside the general in his bronze armour. They were marching away from the mountain into the valley. *Towards us*, Tanner thought. *Good, we have the high ground.* There were others in the army not dressed in black: a crowd of men in blue tunics, and there, in the middle, was Worrick, still carrying his axe.

'How many are there?' Gwen asked.

'Several hundred soldiers at least,' Tanner said. 'They have varkules, and Varlot is with them.' He glanced at their Beasts in the courtyard below. A painted mosaic had been there once – Tanner could still see the faint outline of a circle with a figure in the centre, covered with dirt and weeds. 'General Gor is leading them. They must be after the third piece of the mask. Geffen must have told them where to find it from beyond the grave.' Gwen's brother had seen the secrets of their map, the locations of each piece of the mask. Then he'd betrayed them.

Tanner looked at Rufus. 'Your Beast saved us – if Falkor hadn't warned us, we might not have come out in time.'

'In time for what?' Castor said. 'They're still all the way...' When he looked again, the army was already approaching the stream at the base of the valley. They were moving quickly.

Tanner could hear the faint, sinister clang of the soldiers' boots and weapons. Nervous excitement played in his belly. He was actually looking forward to fighting these men, he realised. Up until now he'd experienced fear, exhilaration, relief, a will to survive – but this thrill of power? *It's the blood*, came a message from Firepos.

Shaking himself, Tanner pointed to the intact right-hand side of the castle, where the tower stood. 'From there, we can use the walls, attack them from above. If we're in danger, we can retreat inside the castle and lose them in the ruins. We'll have an advantage,' Tanner said, hurrying back into the courtyard. He patted Firepos's wing and she dropped her head to Tanner's chest. 'Come on!' he called to them.

Gripping the carved serpent that curled up his staff, Rufus stayed on the wall, looking out, while Gwen and Castor picked their way down. 'So,' Castor called to Tanner, 'When the soldiers get here – what? We ambush them?'

Tanner paused. 'We need more of a plan.' He looked at the ancient outer wall, the mortar worn away and the stones crumbling. Part of it had already collapsed. *Surely one good shove would send the rest of the wall tumbling down the hillside? One good shove...* Tanner pointed. 'We hide behind there and when the first soldiers arrive, we push the wall onto them. They'll be buried and with luck any soldiers following will be held back long enough for us to regroup and hide in the tower. But come on. For now, we need to get high enough to monitor their progress.'

Thunder rumbled overhead and a cold wind whistled through the courtyard. Tanner found a handhold, lifted himself up to a ruined window and hoisted himself through. The first-storey room had collapsed, leaving narrow stone walkways that were hung with vines. Tanner crept along a stone ledge inside the wall until he found narrow arrow-slits overlooking the courtyard.

Castor climbed in beside him. Outside, Gwen called to Rufus, 'Quickly!'

Rufus was still on the outer wall, his back to them.

'Not a bad position,' Castor said.

Lightning flashed over the valley, thunder cracked, and they all jumped. A slow, chilly rain began to fall. Nera came to the castle – the hole was too small for her – and with rippling fur she jumped onto the other side.

'Rufus!' Gwen called again.

Rain hit Tanner and Castor through jagged gaps in the stone ceiling, far overhead.

'Something's wrong,' Rufus said.

Tanner ran back to the window-hole, helped Gwen climb in, and as he climbed out the rain pounded harder and became a sudden downpour. Through slashing rain, Tanner splashed across the courtyard mud, ran up the steps of the wall to Rufus and saw it: the army had turned away. They were marching west, up the slope of another mountain, out of the valley. They were going the wrong way. Had Geffen lied to them about the mask's location? Rufus seemed oblivious to the cold rain, his ragged clothes clinging like a second, filthy skin.

'We have to stop them!' Tanner shouted over the rain. Gor had the other pieces of the mask. Tanner needed them back.

He looked back: Falkor waited motionless with Firepos in the courtyard, and now Castor was running over to see what was happening. Nera and Gulkien perched on the castle, with Gwen watching from inside. Lightning flashed in the valley. *We have to draw them here*, Tanner thought. *This could be our only chance to recover the other mask pieces – but how?* He looked at the army again: in another moment they would be gone. *Think!*

Castor reached the steps and hurried up to join them. 'Wait!' he shouted at the army. His voice disappeared into the rain. 'Come back and fight.'

'Tanner,' Rufus said, 'you have to do something.

They're moving away!' Hair streaking his face, Rufus nodded to Tanner's belt, where he had hidden the mask shard. 'Hurry – put it on! I promise you it will get Gor back here.' He brought his face close to Tanner's and lowered his voice to a whisper. 'Trust me.' Tanner found that he could hardly break his gaze. What was it about this boy? He'd charmed the Beasts from the first time they'd met him, and now... Tanner felt himself bending to Rufus's will.

Castor laughed, interrupting the moment, and wiped water from his face. 'That's ridiculous,' he said, looking at the mask. 'Maybe we can get our Beasts to go after the soldiers.' The rain pelted louder around them, turning the mountainside into slick rivers of mud.

'No,' Tanner said. His eyes were still fixed on Rufus. 'We need to use the cover of the castle. There are too many of them to fight in the open.'

Gwen shouted, 'What are you doing?'

Tanner pressed his drenched hair out of his eyes and held up the mask to show her. Lightning snarled across the sky behind him. In the flash, the wet leather seemed to glow at the edges, as if it was burning white-hot.

'Do it, Tanner!' Rufus said. 'Quickly! It will help, I promise. Gor will sense the mask's power when you wear it and direct his troops back here.' His lips were trembling and he watched Tanner's face intently.

As Tanner lowered the mask, his heart beat frantically. The leather dripped cold rainwater, but the surface seemed to shimmer. *This is wrong*. The fear in Tanner's chest was deep, but... *We have to lure Gor back here. It's our only hope of retrieving the other pieces of the mask*. With both hands, he eased the mask closer to his face. Rain beat the old leather. Tanner felt a thin layer of soft fuzz inside, like the lining of a cured animal skin. Tiny hairs flecked the surface. Tanner closed his eyes. The last thing he heard was Firepos screaming.

No, this cannot happen! I lunge into the rain, wings open, and when I dive, my talons snare the sliver of evil-tainted skin in Tanner's hand. I pull back, ready to toss it into the wind — let it be buried by the mud — but Tanner holds my leg, his grip strong. He is faster now, changed, and he shouts, 'Stop it, Firepos! It's mine!' I twist away into the air, carrying him. Tanner has caught hold of the mask again! It slips through my talons, and Tanner lands in a deep puddle of mud and broken stone.

'I have to!' he shouts, and as I spin to take it back, he presses the flesh-mask to his face.

The army advances

Chapter Eleven

The mask snaps over my face. My skin feels stretched tight, as though bonded to the underside of these twisted features I now look out of. Daylight stretches, squeezing out the colours, turning the world into a cacophony of rushing greys, shadowy whites and deep black. The roar of the rain thunders in my ears. I can see every drop suspended, fast-moving in the air, before it hits with a tiny, noisy spray. There is the rapid surge of blood coursing in my veins and arteries, the tremor of excitement and hunger in the wall of my stomach.

General Gor, I think. Face me!

There's more to me now than the power of a Beast. It feels twisted into lust for battle, the need to fight. I feel a roar emerging from my chest, craning back to call out to the tumultuous sky. Let battle commence! May I spill blood!

But there's something else. I snap round. Rufus stares at me. We look into each other's eyes. He knows something.

Panic seizes me and I grab the mask, pull. It stretches, clinging to my face. I yank with both hands, and the mask pulls free. My face feels numb and I slump to the wet ground.

A steady rain thundered in the courtyard as Castor and Gwen helped Tanner up. Hastily, Tanner slipped the mask beneath his tunic. The mask seemed to channel his new powers and distort them into a vengeful lust for battle. It scared Tanner; had he really called out? But neither Gwen nor Castor said anything and Tanner dared to hope that his shouts to spill blood had only rung out in his head.

He shook the others off and took hold of Rufus's arm, pulling him to one side.

'What did the mask do? What power does it have?' he demanded.

Rufus gave a thin smile. 'What did it do? It brought the soldiers here. It did what you needed it to do.'

As he finished speaking, Castor pointed beyond a broken section of wall and cried out.

'Tanner! The soldiers are coming!'

Tanner and Gwen raced up the wall steps after Castor to stand beside Rufus: in the valley, the army had turned and was marching towards them. The soldiers stomped in the rain like an angry black smear across the landscape. Tanner saw spears and swords glinting, and the varkules' hair standing up in rigid strips down their spines. Most of the men had already crossed the stream and now the men on varkules, led by General Gor, rushed ahead of the rest. Tanner heard Gor shouting, 'Faster! Move, you dogs!' He was carrying a long pole with hooked barbs on the end, like a harpoon, and human skulls shifted at his belt as he moved ever closer.

'He's collecting mementos from his victims!' Gwen gasped. 'What a monster.'

'We have to get ready for the ambush now,' Tanner said, 'before they spot us.'

'What's the plan, fearless leader?' Castor asked.

Tanner had to control the urge to lunge at Castor. Gwen was watching silently, fingers clasping the edge of her cloak to draw it around her body.

'Get behind the outer wall, like I said. Topple it on the first soldiers. Then we can move to higher ground.' He pointed to the tower. 'The Beasts can wait for us there. We'll join them later. Gor will have lost key men, and if Varlot's with him, he'll struggle to pick his way up to a castle on a mountain top because of the narrow paths. We'll have the advantage, and then we attack – together.' He stomped down to the courtyard and tried to smile when he reached Firepos. 'I'm sorry about the mask,' Tanner murmured. 'I was just trying to…' No answering message came back. She lowered her wing to help him climb up.

As Castor went to Nera, he called to Rufus, 'Last chance to leave.'

Rufus hesitated, then readied his staff. Water sluiced down the curled hook at the end. Falkor tasted the rain with his tongue. 'You will need my help against that army,' Rufus said. 'You helped my sister, Castor: I'm with you.'

Castor didn't respond, but his lip curled in a sneer.

Firepos took off, her feathers fluttering in the cold wind, and landed on the edge of the ruined stone roof of the tower. The tower's ceiling had caved in long ago, but the top floor, now thick with moss and ivy, was still intact. Gulkien flew in, and Nera crawled up with Falkor slithering beside her. Rainwater drained through holes in the floor and down a winding, broken staircase to the floors below.

When all the Beasts were inside, Tanner said, 'That's perfect. When we join them, we can fly out of the open roof and attack.'

Gwen touched her axes nervously and nodded to Rufus's hooked serpent-staff. 'These soldiers are killers. Are you sure that weapon will be strong enough?'

'I think so,' he said.

'I know mine will be,' Castor said, and he drew his sword, twirling it on his palm as he paced. His dagger rattled on his belt. 'They don't get to walk away this time.' He pointed at Tanner. 'Agreed?'

Tanner swallowed. He could hear men shouting over the wet panting of varkules.

'No prisoners,' Castor said.

'Castor, just focus,' Gwen said.

'No,' Castor said, still watching Tanner. 'I want to hear our fearless leader say it. We're not going to let them run away this time. We're going to get the mask back and end it here.'

Their Beasts were watching through holes in the tower wall, listening and sniffing at the rain. Tanner heard the beating of Varlot's hooves coming up the mountain, and heard General Gor shouting, 'Move! Towards the castle!'

It was time for them to get into position.

'Come on,' Tanner said. He led the way towards the crumbling outer wall, keeping his body low. The others followed and knelt beside him. Peering through cracks between the stones, they could see the soldiers' approach. Some of them rode varkules, their striped fur glistening as jaws snapped at the air, hungry for blood.

Gwen tested the wall, leaning a shoulder against some of the stones. They didn't shift.

'Are you sure about this, Tanner?' she asked. 'These walls have been here for hundreds of years, even if they are dilapidated. They were built to last.'

Tanner felt a prickle of doubt. He shoved the point of his blade between two of the rocks and twisted, but neither of them gave. And all the time, the army was drawing closer.

'Oh, great,' Castor said. 'We're separated from our Beasts and stuck behind a wall that won't shift. Just great. Why don't we throw our weapons down and step out to greet Gor and his men? Tear open our tunics and show them where to aim their blades?' He shook his head in disgust.

'I can use my magic,' Rufus said quietly. Already, the palms of his hands glowed in anticipation.

'I'm not sure,' Tanner said. There was something about Rufus's tricks that made Tanner feel uneasy, something about the way he'd looked at Tanner when he'd worn the mask. This wizard boy felt like someone he needed to take care around.

There was a shout from below and Gor rushed up the hill, his varkule covered in mud. Through the driving rain, Tanner saw Gor's dragon-helmet, raised off his face: discoloured brown skin covered the right half of Gor's face, curling up and around his jaw. A horn rose from one of the temples, ending in a barbed hook. The mask. General Gor was wearing the other two pieces of the Mask of Death!

The mask will make him stronger, Tanner thought. *Does he feel what I did?* Did Gor get that same rush of bloodlust, did the world come sharply into focus for him too when he donned the mask? If so, Tanner knew he would be fighting a man who would stop at nothing.

Unless he crushed Gor to death now…

'Do it,' he said to Rufus. 'Do whatever you must.'

Instantly, the boy leapt to his feet, his blue tunic snapping in the vicious wind. Soldiers cried out and arrows pierced the air, landing around Tanner and the others.

'What's the little fool trying to do?' Castor whispered as an arrow punctured the grass beside him.

Rufus extended his hands and held his arms above his head. A shimmering ball of light rose up above him. Then with a cry of fury, he sent the ball shooting down into the men below. Arcs of light darted off the ball, exploding into the wall. Gwen scrambled back, pulling at Tanner and Castor.

'Get out of the way!' she cried, understanding what was happening.

The wall smashed into razor-sharp splinters

of rock that shot out across the landscape. Men ducked and cried out as the shards of stone rained down on them, while the shimmering ball of magic rolled between groups cowering behind raised shields. There were cries of agony as Rufus's ball of magic set fire to their tunics or turned their armour red with heat.

Rufus sank down to the ground beside them, his shoulders drooping, but his gaze watching the chaos below.

'That's everything I can do,' he said, sounding drained.

'It's enough,' said Tanner, getting to his feet. It had caused all the chaos he'd hoped for. But Gor had survived. He stood with his feet braced, in the centre of the men.

'Get up, you cowering fools,' he shouted. He glanced over his shoulder at a fresh group of soldiers armed with spears and pikes, bringing up the rear. Varlot was among them. He'd grown huge, his enormous bronze hooves splashing through the mud. His face looked more human than ever and his armour shone. He looked unstoppable.

'Come on, quickly!' Gor called.

Soldiers poured into the courtyard, but Tanner and his friends were already making their way up to the tower. He took his place beside Firepos and watched the rainwater pelt the soldiers' black armour, dripping from their weapons and stinking, slavering varkules. Varlot was among them, moving quickly. He appeared beside the tower, his face grotesquely human, followed by the rest of the army led by Gor. Tanner spotted the blue tunics of Hartwell villagers among the soldiers. *So they've joined forces.* He shouldn't have been surprised – there had been so much hate in that village. Amazingly, none of them had spotted Tanner and his friends creeping into the tower. They still had the element of surprise.

Varlot came closer, but his hooves slipped and struggled to find a hold on the rocky terrain. He stumbled to one side, his massive chest heaving beneath his armour. He sent out a curse of frustration. Tanner could see him panting with the effort. It was just as Tanner had planned; Varlot was at a disadvantage on the sheer mountainside.

Gwen and Rufus mounted their Beasts, but Castor still stood beside Tanner. 'If you mess this up for us...' He didn't finish the sentence.

'We won't lose, I promise you,' Tanner said, avoiding looking at Castor. He didn't want Castor to see the lust for battle in his eyes – a lust brought to him through drinking Firepos's blood, and made even stronger since wearing the mask. Tanner didn't want Castor or Gwen to discover what had happened to him, though he suspected Rufus already knew. That boy... There was more to him than naive, clumsy magic.

'Fan out!' they heard Gor shout. 'Search the castle – you, into the caves! That boy has a piece of the mask. He's taunting me, he brought us here! A reward to the one who finds him!' Gor threw Varlot a glance. 'Keep up!'

Castor clasped Tanner's shoulder. 'Lead us, Tanner.' His mocking had melted away. Even Castor recognised what Tanner felt in his heart – he'd never been more ready to lead them into battle.

Tanner climbed onto Firepos's back. Nera flexed her legs, rippling with muscles, while Gulkien ground his fangs, his leathery wings poised and ready. Even Falkor seemed to be watching Tanner, eager for the fight, with Rufus on his muscular back. Tanner ran his hand along Firepos's shimmering feathers. Water sizzled in steam-bursts as it hit Firepos. More soldiers climbed over the broken wall into the courtyard below. Through the slit windows, Tanner could see that they were armed with narrow swords, crossbows and spears.

'Find him!' Gor shouted. 'If I don't find that mask, the piece he was using, I will make a new mask out of your skins!'

Tanner looked at his friends, then drew his sword. He felt Firepos's heartbeat quicken, and her feathers flared yellow-orange, brilliant and beautiful.

'We're with you,' Gwen said, her face pale.

A dim blue light started in Rufus's fingertips. Steam rose from his hands, sizzling the rain. 'I'm ready,' he said.

Tanner pressed Firepos's feathers, and as she rose, he raised his sword and cried, 'Now!'

Castor's fury

Chapter Twelve

I surge over the ruined lip of the tower and open my wings. As I scream and drop to the courtyard, the soldiers' varkules rear back, snapping their fangs in the cold rain. Their leader, General Gor, knocks his helmet visor down and shouts, 'Kill them all!' A soldier hurls a spear that wobbles in midair and flies wide. I snare his varkule and toss them both into more soldiers, biting another one. On my right, Nera lunges into a mass of them, who yell and collide in a whirl of fur and metal. Falkor, our new ally, slithers close with his Chosen Rider, and when a varkule rider readies a spear, Falkor flashes in and out again in a blur: the rider is down and the varkule hobbles back, its front legs crushed. Falkor hisses, his red eyes shining through the pounding rain, and now Rufus's hands tremble with light.

When the soldiers attack, I beat my wings in a thunder-rain spray that knocks them back. I take off, spear a soldier with my beak and grab two more in my talons, yanking them free of their saddles, flying high, and then I hurl them into the front lines of the advancing army. I circle fast to dive in a rush that makes Tanner cling tightly to my neck. We are one, Tanner and I. My blood and strength flows in his veins. I can feel excitement in his touch. We fight together; my heart should swell with pride. Yet a cloud of darkness hovers over me. Tanner should never have worn that mask; he does not understand the power it yields.

We join Gulkien, Nera and Falkor to slam the army back against the ruined castle wall. As I connect, the soldiers shout in terror, their varkules scrambling to get away, colliding in a chaos of bodies and weapons against the stone. They break like a wave into a writhing mound.

There are more behind me, led by Varlot, rushing through the wall gap. Varlot stumbles but there is General Gor, on top of the wall, shouting orders, directing the counter-attack. More soldiers – and Hartwell villagers in blue – hurry to surround us. I grab a fallen varkule in my beak, it snarls and flails, and I toss it into the incoming soldiers. They go down in a wall of puddle water, but more men quickly take their place. I cry out and beat my wings in the freezing water: make war! My friends answer and attack.

From Firepos's back, Tanner leant into the jumble of wounded soldiers, striking and stabbing. During the ambush, they had pinned the courtyard soldiers in a stampede of confusion against the ruined outer wall, but in another moment the rest of the army would arrive, and most of these soldiers were still alive and full of panic. Tanner had to get close to Gor and the mask he was wearing. When a soldier in the pile blocked with his spear, Tanner pulled his sword back, then lunged for the man. The soldier's varkule snapped at Tanner but Firepos lanced its head with her beak.

From Tanner's right came a low war cry. He looked back: Nera and Castor were on that flank, and now a mass of soldiers and villagers rushed them on foot, swarming the courtyard. Castor urged Nera directly into them, and she pounced, claws and teeth bared. She broke a hole in the centre of the line, with Castor stabbing and hacking from her back. Soldiers rushed her, surrounding Castor and Nera in a circle of spears.

Nera swiped, the soldiers dodged back, and when Castor batted down an incoming spear, another lanced past his face.

Blue light streaked past, hit the soldiers on Nera's left, and they exploded in a sudden cloud of burning armour, blood and black-stone spray. Another beam shot high in a trail of steam. Rufus was shaking on Falkor's back, his jaw set, the veins in his neck taut like tense ropes. His hands were glowing again. Falkor flicked the rain with his tongue, and when a soldier rushed past Nera, closing on them, Falkor snapped forward, then back. The soldier slumped and went down, his neck broken.

'Look out, Tanner!' Gwen shouted.

A crowd of villagers in blue tunics surrounded Firepos, three with crossbows aimed at her. She beat her wings: one tripped, Tanner tackled another, and Gwen sent her axe spinning into the third villager's chest. Tanner rolled with the villager over the slippery stone, and as the man's crossbow shot into the air, Tanner shoved his sword into the man's shoulder. Tanner saw an axe reflected in his blade and he rolled, yanking his sword free.

On his feet, Tanner spun. Worrick whipped his axe at Tanner's throat but Tanner blocked, his sword scraping down the other man's blade. The force shook Worrick's whole body but Tanner's sword held. The force should have knocked Tanner wide, but his feet stayed planted where they were and he could feel his muscles working hard as he leant into the attack, bringing his face close. Worrick's eyes were wide, confused.

'What's happened to you?' the man managed to gasp. 'You once told me you didn't want to fight and now you can't wait to kill me!'

In reply, Tanner yanked the sword down hard, shoving the axe into the ground, and he punched Worrick in the gut. Worrick stumbled, raised his hands – 'Wait—'

Tanner hesitated, resisting the blood lust that

coursed through him. Worrick was at his mercy — fear burned in his eyes. Tanner wanted to kill him. *It's because of the mask,* Tanner thought. Fighting the urge, he hit Worrick's temple with his sword hilt, knocking him out cold. But the fury still raged through him.

Looking back over the heads of the villagers and soldiers, he saw Firepos watching him. Tanner's sword, his hands, even his chin were smeared with blood. A soldier came at Tanner from behind. Tanner spun, caught the man's wrist to stop his sword, but the force knocked Tanner backwards and the soldier's blade was at his throat. Firepos's shadow loomed over them. She beat her wings and threw the screaming soldier over her back. Tanner shoved the villagers aside, and as he reached for Firepos's wing Rufus shouted, 'Stand back!' as a blue beam exploded between them. The scream of hot stone and rainwater threw Tanner backwards. He glimpsed Rufus's face, frozen in horror — and Tanner landed in a deep puddle of grey-red water that convulsed with raindrops. He picked himself up, his hand brushing someone else's fingers: a severed hand. Tanner rolled the other way, towards a dead varkule, and as he stood, armoured soldiers rushed him with spears and swords.

'Where's the mask?' one of them cried. Tanner had to resist the urge to feel his tunic, to make sure the mask was still hidden there.

'Go and help Castor!' he shouted to Rufus.

The men were drawing closer. He flashed his sword down to parry a blade, spun, and kicked it out of the soldier's hands, then drove his sword at the man. More spears lanced behind him and Tanner dived, pulling his sword free. The soldier went down clutching his chest. *He never had a chance*, Tanner thought. *Not now I've worn the mask*.

A club hit Tanner's sword, knocking it away. The soldiers scattered. Varlot, his bronze armour streaked with rain, stepped over Tanner. Varlot's skin was tight with muscle under his armour.

There were no scars or marks, nothing from their last fight. Varlot's club was studded with jagged, irregular points, like razorblades. Tanner found his sword in a pool of bloody rain.

Varlot's voice rumbled and wheezed. Tanner heard words in the noise: 'Not so fast, are you?'

On Tanner's right, past a mass of soldiers, Castor was still fighting on Nera's back.

'I will break you,' Varlot said. The evil Beast had grown used to negotiationg the rocky terrain, it seemed. As Tanner stumbled back, Varlot followed.

The pieces of the mask, Tanner thought. *I need to get them. Where is General Gor?* He looked back. *Where?*

Behind Tanner, soldiers had surrounded the others. Varlot's club snapped the side of Tanner's head, knocking him to the ground. His vision blurred, his head ringing, bleeding. When Varlot swung again, Tanner rolled under it. He caught Varlot's arm in a chink between the plates of armour near his elbows. Varlot howled and stomped. Tanner dodged a bronze hoof, but another blurred past his head and grazed his face, sending Tanner spinning back. He staggered, and Varlot screamed, 'Kill him! Kill that boy!'

Soldiers cut Tanner off from behind, readying their swords. Varlot swung again, and Tanner blocked, but the force threw him backwards. Soldiers came at him, and Tanner dived back at Varlot, rolling under the club and swinging again. Varlot pulled back, Tanner missed, and the soldiers surrounded him.

As Tanner dodged a sword and struck back, he saw Varlot lean low to speak to a soldier – smaller than the others – dressed in black cloth, not armour. Fabric covered all but the slender soldier's eyes. The masked soldier darted through a gap in the fighting, towards Gwen; he half-hobbled, his left shoulder dragging lower than his right. Tanner saw white skin on his hand like the side of a rotting fish. The masked soldier drew a black dagger and slipped into the crowd where Gwen fought beside Gulkien.

Tanner knocked the soldiers back. 'Gwen!' he shouted.

She spun, confused – the masked soldier drove the blade at her chest – Gwen caught his wrist, and as he pushed her off-balance, his pale hand grasped for her neck, the fingers opening and closing – he was searching for the locket!

'Help!' Gwen screamed. 'Tanner!'

Tanner hit the surrounding soldiers from behind, knocking them aside with fast stabs of his sword. They landed near where Gwen grappled with her attacker. Tanner grabbed the masked soldier's shoulder but it seemed to cave in under his fingers. The flesh slipped and pulled free in Tanner's hand. A sharp, putrid smell filled the air: his hand was smeared with black clumps of skin and hair and wet, lumpy blood that congealed and dropped in blobs. Tanner's stomach heaved. Gwen screamed and wrestled with the attacker onto the hard, wet stone.

Tanner spotted a shadow and he lunged aside, and Varlot's club struck the ground in a blast of stone and bloody water. As Tanner circled, Varlot swiped again. Tanner blocked, fell backwards, and rolled when Varlot stomped at his head. Hands slippery and shaking, Tanner scrambled backwards through puddles of mud. Tanner spotted General Gor past Varlot, on the ramparts of the outer wall.

'You die,' Varlot rumbled. 'Sport for crow and worm.'

Varlot attacked again, Tanner dodged, tried to hit him, but in a flash of hooves Tanner was forced back, panting. *He's too big*, Tanner thought. *Too fast. I can't get close enough to hit him. What if I put on the mask?* Tanner's fingers brushed his belt, where the piece was hidden inside his tunic. *No. What if I put it on and never want to take it off?*

Lightning flashed: a shadow lunged behind Varlot. Nera slammed into him with Castor on her back, and as Nera jumped away, Castor called, 'Tanner!' and lobbed a spear. It struck the dirt at Tanner's feet.

'Press forward!' General Gor called. The two adjoining pieces of the mask clung to the left side of his face and chin, like skin with the colour burnt from it.

Soldiers rushed to cut off Nera. Tanner put his sword away and grabbed the spear in both hands. Near the castle, Falkor and Rufus were surrounded; behind Tanner, Firepos still fought; and Gulkien snarled near Gwen to keep the soldiers away as she struggled with her masked attacker. *No time*, Tanner thought. 'Varlot!' he called.

Varlot's voice rasped, 'I enjoy...'

'No more.' Tanner jabbed the spear but Varlot batted it aside. Tanner twisted the spear free and stabbed again: he hit Varlot's chest armour with a chink that drove Varlot back a step. Tanner stabbed again, but Varlot blocked once, twice, and on the third thrust, Tanner drew his sword with one hand and lunged, driving it into Varlot's wrist.

The blade cut deep. Varlot bellowed, dropped his club, and Tanner ran the spear into the base of Varlot's mask. The armour-edge cut against the spear so the point sliced wide in a bloody gash, and as Tanner moved in with his sword, Varlot's body contorted, shrank. The human part – his arms and chest – were sinking in, becoming a horse's neck, and his faceless mask stretched long into an animal head. *He's wounded*, Tanner realised. *He's losing his strength, shrinking. But for how long?* Tanner already knew Varlot had the ability to heal himself.

Varlot punched, and when Tanner ducked, he jabbed his spear left. Varlot dodged right, into Tanner's sword. The blade sliced through the rain towards Varlot's exposed neck. He was about to defeat the evil Beast once and for all, when the world flashed white. Fire flooded Tanner's skull. *Firepos!* Something was happening to his Beast. Tanner heard himself screaming as he fell to his knees.

Blinking through the pain, Tanner saw Firepos on the outer wall, facing General Gor. The General raised his barbed harpoon into the rain and shouted a wordless war cry. Firepos writhed, as if something had lodged under her wing in the scar where her feathers had been ripped – as if it were dragging her down.

It's the old scar. It pains me again. Tanner could see his companion struggling to spread her wings, failing to hook the general with her beak. Despite her great size, she looked vulnerable as her feathers turned a dull brown. The light in her eyes grew dim and fresh pain throbbed in Tanner's head. Somehow, Derthsin had sent his evil power to hurt Firepos – and Tanner, too. Just in time to help them lose this battle.

Across the space between them, Tanner looked into the Flame Bird's wide, terrified eyes. *I'm sorry,* she seemed to say.

Battle for the mask

Chapter Thirteen

I thrash as white-hot barbs sink deeper under my wing, in the scar. When I move, pain floods my mind. General Gor laughs, his harpoon aimed at my neck, but he is not looking at me. Below, Tanner has his sword at Varlot's throat. Somehow, Tanner has beaten that unnatural Beast – he broke Varlot and is ready to finish it, even as my pain snaps through the rain and shocks him.

Tanner tries to blink away the fire, but I know he feels it. I am so close to General Gor – I can crush him with my beak – but when I straighten, the invisible snares bite hard. I cry out. The stench of evil magic tastes like mould. This is not Gor's doing. He is a soldier, that's all. This is old magic. As the scar drags me down, pain blocks everything out, and when I shriek, I see Tanner double over in the courtyard, soaked and dripping. He looks at me, desperate. I'm sorry, I think. I am so sorry.

Tanner held his sword to Varlot's neck and grimaced at the flashes of pain that spotted his vision. He gasped misty breaths of rain, the cold water pounding in steady sheets, but nothing could dampen the lust for battle that still enflamed him.

General Gor laughed. 'Well done, boy. But you cannot kill Varlot.'

Behind Tanner, he heard the clicking slither of Falkor approaching.

'Let's find out,' Tanner said. Blood trickled down Varlot's chest, but in another moment, the Beast would heal. *I have to do this now*, Tanner thought.

'Lord Derthsin has your Beast,' General Gor said, nodding to Firepos. 'Derthsin can smash her like an insect. His hold over her, through old scars, is great. Your Beast never should have carried him to the volcano.'

Tanner clenched his fists. Anger welled in his chest. The pain only made it worse, and when Firepos struggled again Tanner pressed the blade deeper into Varlot's neck. 'I'll cut his throat!' Varlot's nostrils flared, but he knew better than to fight while he still dripped blood and Tanner held his blade close to his throat.

Gor smiled. 'You don't understand. Now drop your sword, boy.'

There must be a way, Tanner thought, and he looked around frantically. In the raging storm, Castor and Nera had beaten back the soldiers, but Tanner couldn't see what was happening in the mass of soldiers around Gwen and Gulkien. There must be...

Rufus stepped beside Tanner, raised his glowing hand to Firepos. Firepos saw him too, and when she buckled, Tanner reached out to stop Rufus. 'No!' Too late: a beam of blue light jetted out of Rufus's fingers, scalding the rain, jolting Rufus backwards. The light flashed past Firepos's face in an explosion of white sparks that knocked General Gor back and sent Firepos screeching into the air. She screamed a surprised, thrilling war cry. She was free!

In the blast, the soldiers scattered, and Varlot,

whose armour had melted back to a horse's glossy coat, kicked free of Tanner and charged for a gap in the wall. *I have to let him go*, Tanner thought, sprinting across the courtyard to the steps. He bounded up onto the outer wall. The mask was all that mattered.

As Tanner reached the top, General Gor said, 'You poor little fool. You have no idea...'

Tanner pivoted, feet steady on the slippery stone, and when Gor's harpoon came down, Tanner grabbed it and yanked. Gor stumbled forward, and Tanner drove his sword into Gor's face: the blade caught the edge of his cheek, splitting the two mask pieces in a bloody gash. Gor screamed, reached up, but Tanner's hand was already there. He caught the dangling mask. Gor punched Tanner's shoulder, but Tanner didn't let go, and both pieces of the mask ripped away. Tanner staggered back, his shoulder throbbing.

Three pieces, Tanner thought. *I've got them. There's only one more left!* General Gor touched the cheek wound and glanced at his bloody fingertips. When he looked back at Tanner, Gor's eyes had changed. He smiled, as if he was impressed. As if Tanner was suddenly more interesting. Without lowering his sword, Tanner slipped the blood-smeared mask pieces into his tunic, alongside the one he already had. Gor didn't speak, just smiled and slowly backed away, towards the edge of the wall. His arms and legs throbbing with exhaustion, Tanner followed. Firepos was safe, soaring high above him.

The general climbed onto the rampart, his back to the mountain slope on the other side. 'Retreat!' he yelled at his soldiers. 'Fall back!'

Castor was shouting, but Tanner couldn't make out the words through the rain. He saw Gwen circling the masked attacker in the mud below. *She needs help*, Tanner thought. *One of us has to get down there.*

Icy water dripped down Tanner's neck. His joints ached, stiff and raw. He glanced at Castor again. He was standing over a body, his dagger clutched in a hand.

'Go to Gwen!' Tanner called over. 'You're closer than I am.' Castor spotted her stand-off with the man in the mask, then sent Tanner a swift nod and began leaping over rocks towards her.

And now to finish you, Tanner thought, focussing on Gor.

The general chuckled. 'Someday,' he said, 'someday I will kill you.' Before Tanner had a chance to do anything, the general stepped off into the empty air. Tanner rushed to the wall: on the mountainside below, General Gor had landed on his varkule's back. He was already riding away, surrounded by soldiers. And there was Varlot beside him. 'You don't know what's coming, boy!' Gor called. 'You can't win!'

Tanner ran for the steps. The army was retreating. The soldiers were scattering in every direction, escaping out of the gaps in the perimeter wall.

'...getting away!' Castor shouted, from where he stood beside Gwen. He had the tip of his sword trained on the masked soldier, who stood at a safe distance, his own weapon braced before his body. Gwen held an axe in each hand, her face unmoving as she stared at the man they'd cornered.

Tanner jumped down the steps three at a time. 'I know,' Tanner said. 'Finish him!' He pointed his sword at the masked soldier.

Suddenly, Gwen shouted. While Tanner had been talking, the masked soldier had lunged towards her, pinning her to the mud. Castor didn't dare throw his dagger, for fear of harming Gwen. Gulkien leapt forward to help, and Gwen shoved her attacker back, rolling across the courtyard. In the skirmish, she lost the axes she'd been holding. The others glinted at her waist – useless there. She had no chance to bring them out and her cloak was twisted around her waist, making it impossible to retrieve her hidden rapier.

'He needs to die!' Tanner shouted angrily, and he

ran with Castor to Gwen. Firepos and Nera were cawing and pacing nearby, as Gulkien snapped at the masked attacker and pulled back, afraid of biting Gwen.

'I'll stop this,' Castor said. He jumped in, grabbed the masked attacker from behind. The soldier jammed his head back into Castor's nose, and Castor fell backwards in the mud, his face covered in blood.

Rufus and Falkor came to Tanner. 'What in all of Avantia is happening?' Rufus asked.

'What does it look like?' Tanner snapped as he helped Castor up.

Gwen and the attacker rolled close. Tanner aimed his sword, but they were moving too fast, even with his new abilities. He couldn't risk hitting Gwen. The masked soldier slammed Gwen onto her back again, pinning her. She cried out. He grabbed her locket, and as he started to pull, she kicked him off. His hand caught her throat. When they started to fall, Gwen pulled back, let the locket break free – the attacker's grip loosened and she drove her axe into his chest. The masked soldier collapsed. One of his legs twisted the wrong way, as if the joint had been broken. Gwen pried her locket out of his hand – her axe still planted in his chest, like a tree stump.

Rufus stepped closer to Gwen. 'Who was that?'

Gwen fitted the locket back onto her necklace and slipped it under her tunic. Tanner noticed how badly her hands trembled.

'Just a soldier,' Castor said. 'Come on. We've got what we needed – the mask. Let's get off this mountain.'

Tanner nodded and started to turn. Gwen cried out. It was a high, feral noise, as if she'd been stabbed. *He's not dead*, Tanner thought, and he ran back.

Gwen had peeled back the folds of the attacker's mask, and now she slumped over him, sobbing. Gulkien growled over her.

'What?' Castor said. 'Is she hurt? Gwen?'

She shook and beat her fist on the soldier's chest.

Tanner took Gwen's shoulders and gently eased her away from the body. She was smeared with blood and bits of rotting skin. Tanner saw it: the soldier's face was bloody, missing sections of flesh exposing his cheekbones and grinning teeth, but Tanner still recognised the blue eyes and round chin.

'I'm sorry,' Tanner said. Gwen was still crying, hysterical.

It was her brother, Geffen.

At last, Geffen dies

Chapter Fourteen

As Tanner led Gwen away, Castor grabbed her axe and pulled it from Geffen's chest. Tanner shuddered and turned away. Now that the battle was over, he'd lost his lust for blood. Through gaps in the wall, he could see soldiers retreating at the bottom of the valley. *They could already be on their way to the next piece of the mask*, he thought. But he was too exhausted to chase after them. Nera came to Castor, but as he grabbed her fur to climb up, Geffen stirred.

'Stand back!' Tanner shouted.

Gwen shook Tanner away and ran to her brother. She crouched at Geffen's side. He coughed blood and started to sit up. The veins in his neck were green, pulsing with rot. Gulkien bared his fangs and pushed between Geffen and Gwen. Nera growled beside Firepos, and Falkor hissed low, his eyes locked on Geffen.

'He is full of evil magic,' Rufus said. 'It has

brought him back from the dead. He is no longer one of us.'

Castor glanced at Rufus. 'Thanks, I think we can all see that.'

Geffen reached for Gwen, and Tanner drew his sword. 'Gwen!'

She took Geffen's hand. 'It's all right. Geffen, can you hear me?'

His head hung slack on his neck, his flesh wet and crumbling in the rain. 'Sorry.' His voice stretched. 'Gwen...'

She pulled him close, and he slumped onto her knee. 'It'll be all right,' she said. 'We'll fix this, we'll find a way. What did he do to you?'

Geffen drew her hand to his chest, and when he pressed her palm flat, blood oozed through his black tunic.

'I don't understand,' she said. 'Why don't I feel your heartbeat? Geffen, tell me what to do.'

'He...took my life,' Geffen said. 'He took my heart and he...laughed.'

Gwen fought back tears. 'It'll be fine. We're stronger than him. We can find a way...'

'I think,' Geffen said. 'I think...I died. He woke me... I was sleeping, dead... He wanted your locket... He wanted you to see me like this. All I feel is *pain*...'

'No,' Gwen said. 'You're alive, you're talking!'

Slowly, Geffen pulled away from her and climbed to his feet. His joints cracked as he tried to steady himself. Gwen looked at Tanner, Castor and Rufus. 'What can we do?' she cried. 'Help me! Geffen, sit down!' She held his hand, as Geffen hobbled towards a gap in the wall. 'Please listen to me...'

'I am sorry,' he said. 'You are stronger. You have to stay alive, Gwen.'

'No, we can help you!'

At the edge of the courtyard, Geffen twisted away from her and staggered over the blocks through the hole in the wall. They ran after him, and as Tanner came through the wall, he saw

Gwen chasing her brother to the edge of the mountain. Geffen climbed onto a ledge: a cliff overlooking a straight drop to sharp rocks far below. Gwen screamed in the rain. Geffen looked back at her, said something, and stepped off: he disappeared over the side. Tanner caught Gwen as she raced after him.

'No!' she shouted. 'He's alive!'

Tanner held Gwen at the ledge. Below, Geffen's body was a black smudge, broken on the rocks. Tanner pulled her back and Castor came to them, Rufus behind him. Castor touched Gwen's shoulder, and she slumped to the rock.

Gulkien edged past Tanner, sat at Gwen's side and reared back to howl. Gwen stroked Gulkien's fur, staring blankly over the ledge. She glanced back and saw Rufus leaning against the castle wall, Falkor at his side. The rain began to thin, and the clouds were giving way to night stars over the distant mountains.

'It's all right,' Tanner said. They were all bloody,

bruised, soaked through, and caked in mud. 'Rufus, we understand if you and your Beast have been through enough. If you want to go back, we can show you the way to Colton so you can find your sister.'

Falkor flicked his tongue and hissed low, as if he didn't like the taste of Tanner's words. Firepos sat on the outer wall, watching over them, and Nera paced behind Castor, her eyes on the valley below, as if she were impatient to move on.

Rufus smiled grimly. 'No, I can't go. There's nothing there for me.' He waved his hand, and in the rain, Tanner saw a vision of the low slope of a pasture, and there was the girl, Isadora, carrying her sack of food. The image danced and swam. Rufus's sister paused at the top of the hill and waved to people in the near-distance, where Tanner could see the outline of Colton. Rufus lowered his hand: the picture was gone.

Castor said, 'Why didn't you tell us you could do that?'

'You didn't ask,' Rufus said. 'But you saw: my sister is safe for now. If I go back, it would endanger her. She's better off without me.' He approached Tanner, and the rain stopped. 'Give me the mask, Tanner.'

Castor stepped close to Rufus, bristling. 'Who do you think you are? You can't just demand the pieces. We've fought hard for those and we follow Tanner, not you!'

This was the first time Tanner had ever heard Castor swear his loyalty to him. Despite their differences, Tanner found himself smiling with pleasure. His body was stiff, muscles sore and blood streaked his skin – but for a moment, the fleeting warmth of happiness moved over him. *I never thought I'd hear Castor swearing allegiance*, he thought.

'I am a wizard,' Rufus said simply. 'And I'm stronger than any of you – even if I don't always look it. The mask will be safest with me. The pieces are too dangerous for you to hold, Tanner.'

He held out a hand, palm up, and waited. Rufus's eyes were locked on Tanner's and Tanner found it hard to look away.

'You told me to wear it,' Tanner said. 'It was your idea.' Some instinct told him that this boy knew more about the mask than he was letting on.

Rufus nodded. 'In the time of greatest need, yes. But the pieces are too strong for a boy, for a mere mortal like you.'

As Castor burst into laughter, Tanner said, 'A mere mortal?'

Gwen said, 'Tanner...'

'No! What do you mean, Rufus? Do you think I'm weak?'

Rufus shrugged. 'I'm sorry, Tanner.'

Castor raised his sword. 'If you're so powerful, let's find out what happens when I stick this sword down your—'

'Stop it!' Gwen said. 'Tanner, give him the mask.' She gave him a long, hard look. 'We know what Firepos's blood has done to you. And don't think I didn't notice how you fought today. You couldn't wait to get into that battle,' she said quietly. 'Wearing that mask helped us today, but it's best that someone else looks after it, Tanner. You know that.'

'You're right,' he admitted. Tanner found the three pieces. He held them up: they were ragged, soggy from the rain and blood-streaked. When he held them together like this, they covered all but his forehead and a strip down the centre of the nose. The mask was almost complete. 'We almost have it,' Tanner said. 'The mask is...'

'I know,' Rufus said.

No you don't, Tanner thought. *I could put the mask on, return to that grey world and never take it off.*

A sense of danger ran through him. *Give him the pieces.* That was Firepos. She'd never tried to tell Tanner what to do before, only guided him. But he gave the pieces to Rufus, who slipped them into his tunic; they vanished into the fabric.

Castor sighed and stepped back to the edge of the cliff. 'The soldiers have gone,' he said.

The rainclouds were clearing, but the sun had gone down and the sky was opening into blackness and stars. The valley stream was overflowing, and Tanner looked back at the bodies piled in deep puddles of mud.

'There's only one more piece,' Tanner said. 'We almost have the whole mask.' He tried to sound hopeful, but none of them looked back at him. They were all tired, staring at the valley and distant mountains. Tanner couldn't see Gwen's face, didn't want to. *We've given up so much*, Tanner thought. *What else can we possibly sacrifice?*

'Where is this going to end?' Castor said. He frowned back at Tanner. 'Down there, with Geffen? Is that where we're going?'

They all watched Tanner, waiting.

'Do you trust me?' Tanner said, and when no one spoke, he said, 'Do you love your homes, your families?'

Gwen said, 'Of course we trust you.'

'We have to fight together,' Tanner said. 'We have three pieces of the mask, but there's one more. Derthsin knows we have them now. Do any of you think he's going to let us find the last piece? If we've pushed him back, he'll only fight harder. We had a saying in my village, "Beware the cornered dog".'

'What are we going to do, Tanner?' Castor asked.

'We're going to win,' Tanner said more loudly. 'We're going to end all of this. It's time.'

Castor glanced at Gwen and Rufus, and crossed his arms. 'Time for what?' he said.

Tanner looked at Firepos, Nera, Gulkien and Falkor, and he felt the slow tension again, as if their lives were strings waiting to be cut.

'What is it?' Gwen said.

Could he tell them what he'd seen when he'd worn the mask? The dark shadows, the screams for help, the heartbeat slowing? 'I've glimpsed death.

I think, I think... One of our Beasts,' Tanner said, and he wiped the rain from his hair. His hands smelt like blood. 'One of them will die.'

He turned his back on them and gazed out over Avantia. No one said a word – what could be said? Out there were General Gor and Vendrake. Varlot was still alive. And Tanner remembered the man he'd glimpsed in fiery visions, talking to Gor: Derthsin.

Tanner shuddered. Death was waiting. The evil warlord had a hold over Firepos through the ancient scar. And now Firepos's blood ran in Tanner's veins. What did that mean for the two of them?

'But I have hope,' he murmured. 'I can't stop believing.' Tanner and his friends had come so far. Only one more piece of mask to find, and then...would Avantia be free of evil?

Castor and Rufus stood beside Tanner. Gwen put her hand on his shoulder. 'Stay strong,' she said.

Tanner smiled. 'Always.'

As I perch on the ruined wall and watch him speak, I feel Tanner's heartbeat — my heartbeat. Tanner has a Beast's blood in his heart, making him strong. But this makes me weak, too — I have lost the power to heal myself.

And now my companion has worn a piece of the mask. Combined with the Beast blood that runs through his veins, this makes him a warrior with rich tastes — my boy enjoys the fight like never before. This is dangerous, and I fear for the future. Will Tanner's quest be his undoing?

Tanner smiles up at me, his eyes proud and shining. He believes that he is strong enough to win. Death is waiting for us, I can feel it watching overhead. But we have to continue together.

Tanner thinks, We won't stop until Derthsin is beaten.

I send a message back: while my heart beats, I am by your side. Always.

He will need me. We our greatest challenge yet. Tanner is a hero, bloody and exhausted, but a hero. Still, he does not yet understand all that he is fighting. Derthsin, Vendrake, Varlot… These are enemies whose strength is growing, just as Tanner's courage swells. And me? My strength *fades by the day. I must dig deep within me, and call on the aid of my Beast friends, to face this new dawn.*

Avantia is on the cusp of great things or eternal ruin. One boy and his friends will decide which way the fates swing. Four Beasts will fight alongside them.

It is time to stand strong. We are about to travel to the heart of evil...

The Chronicles of Avantia

Tanner's story continues in *Fire and Fury*.

The four Riders and their Beasts have been united. But time is fast running out as Derthsin's armies pillage the land with fire and sword.

Will the combined powers of the Beasts and their Riders be enough to save Avantia? Will Tanner succumb to the lure of the mask? The legend of the war for Avantia is about to reach its final, shattering conclusion!

Read on for an exciting preview of *Fire and Fury*, the next adventure in the Chronicles of Avantia...

Chapter One

The thick clouds make the sky the colour of steel. Lightning flashes above and thunder growls like a giant woken from sleep. Cold needles of rain drive against my wings as I soar over forest and plain. Yet the water doesn't chill me. Nothing can quench the ever-burning fire of a Phoenix.

I've watched the sun loop across the sky three times since our battle with Derthsin's minions: the dragon-helmeted General Gor and his horse-Beast, Varlot. Still I hear the sound of clashing metal and war cries beneath the walls of the ruined castle, still I smell the fear of men in my feathers, and still I taste their blood on my beak.

Nera unfolds her long stride below us, her ears flattened and amber eyes flashing. Her sodden fur ripples gold and brown under the lightning that illuminates the plain. Between her shoulder-blades, Castor crouches, his hands gripping her fur. At my side, Gulkien stirs the mists in great draughts with his wings of bone and stretched skin. Droplets of spray scatter from his bristling grey coat, and his long nostrils flare as they suck in damp air. He carries the fair-haired girl, Gwen. Her face is set hard and her eyes are narrowed to slits against the wind. In the recesses of the cloak that whips and flaps around her, the silver of her throwing axes glitters.

The weight on my own back shifts a fraction as Tanner grips my flanks tighter with his knees. How long have we have flown together, my Chosen Rider and I? I feel his heartbeat as if it were the pulse of my own hot blood. The bond was between us even before the day when Derthsin slayed Tanner's father. Our bond was forged in the fires of the past, when Fate decreed the Beasts of Avantia should each have a Chosen Rider. But now we are closer than we have ever been before — my blood flows in Tanner's veins, after he drank from the phial given to him by the medicine woman. Pain twists deep inside me. He should never have done that! But it is too late now; he is changing.

Tanner lays the flat of his palm gently against the

feathers on my back, and I hear his voice, somewhere deep in the fibres of my being:

Can we trust him?

I know of whom he speaks, and tip my head to gaze at the fourth of our number – the final companion, who we have known for the shortest time. Falkor slithers as fast as Nera, her long serpent's body pulsing between the tall grasses, tasting the air with her tongue. Her scales, slick with moisture, shimmer purple, black and blue. As she plunges into a dense patch of forest, I have a brief glimpse of the newest Rider, seated behind the jutting spines on my fellow Beast's head, the one whose loyalty Tanner doubts – Rufus. He holds the pieces of the mask. Can we put our faith in him?

Time will tell, I send to Tanner.

Falkor has chosen him, as I have chosen Tanner, and as the others have been drawn to their mortal companions. I should not question another Beast.

Tanner sends more words to me. We should land, Firepos.

With a screech, I dip my wings to bring us into a

long glide downwards. The forest blurs as my talons rip through the upper branches. A clearing rushes towards us.

Yes, time will tell.

The Chronicles of Avantia
books 1 and 2

First Hero
Out Now!

Chasing Evil
Out Now!

The Chronicles of Avantia
book 4

Fire and Fury
Out July 2011

Other great books by
Adam Blade

The Pirate King
Available March 2011!

Ravira Ruler of the Underworld
Out now!

www.beastquest.co.uk